Kiss Me in Fire Station Lane

Mayton Hearts, Volume 2

Abigail Bay

Published by Lady Hatwick, 2025.

This book is dedicated to Megan,

who helps to keep my story straight.

Note from the Author

This book is written for mature readers. *Kiss Me in Fire Station Lane* joins my Mayton Hearts series alongside *Come Back to Bed, Beautiful*. These stories are stand-alone romances so you can join the series anywhere.

For this story I was inspired by a little street in the Hutt Valley called Fire Station Lane, which struck me as the perfect setting for a romance so I fictionalised it and brought it to Mayton!

Johnny Best was only mentioned once in *Come Back to Bed, Beautiful*. He was such a nice guy I thought he deserved his own story. Quinn is a new arrival to Mayton, though she knew Johnny back when they were both fifteen. Locals Kate and Linc, Olive, Lollie and the band pop in to say hello. In true Mayton style, we also have Olive's coffee window, Linc's horses, dogs and small boys creating mayhem.

Please note Mayton and its characters are fictional; any perceived resemblance to known persons or events, past or present, is coincidental. No AI has been used.

Enjoy the read!

Ab.

Kiss Me in Fire Station Lane
Book 2, Mayton Hearts series

Published by AG Spiers imprint Lady Hatwick,
Wellington, New Zealand
Cover design by AG Spiers
ISBN 978-1-06706-600-0 (EPUB)
ISBN 978-1-06706-601-7 (softcover POD)
Requests to publish work from this book should be made to:
abigailbay.author@gmail.com

Prologue

"Kiss me." I didn't stop to think. This is just something you say when you are both fifteen, standing under a streetlight on a hot summer night, and the hot guy in front of you is looking, well, really hot. It's got to be said, so I do.

"Here?" Johnny looks stunned.

"Yes here, in Fire Station Lane." I smile in a way that I hope looks sexy. Alluring? At least mischievous. I don't really expect him to kiss me.

And sadly, he doesn't.

Instead, he flushes bright red and takes a step back, looking stricken. I know I'm no supermodel but I'm also not a complete antidote (yes, I've been reading my mother's historical romances) so Johnny's reaction seems extreme. I'm *sure* he likes me. He is kind and funny, has a killer smile and laughs at my jokes. Have I read him completely wrong?

From across Main Street, behind me, someone calls, "Go on, Johnny, kiss her! You know you want to."

My heart sinks. Now I know why he's so embarrassed. I turn to see his brother lounging against his car in front of their house, watching us with interest. At eighteen, Johnny's brother is three years older and a million times cooler and now I blush, too. I hope he can't see that from across the street. Because I might want to kiss Johnny in Fire Station Lane, but Mario is the kind of guy who'd do a whole lot more than kissing. Mario has the hottest car in town, a smile to die for, and a body like the Farnese Hercules (I've also been reading up on art history).

"Never mind," I say. "It was just a stupid joke." I spin and walk back up the lane, fast. I feel hot all over with shame and embarrassment.

Johnny says something indeterminate, a kind of protesting croak, and Mario laughs. "You missed your moment, little bro. I can see you need coaching. You should come out with me on Friday night, you know, learn from the expert."

Johnny's voice deepens to a growl. I don't want to see them fight because these two are always coming to cuffs and Johnny always loses. I fling through my grandfather's garden gate and around his cottage to the oak tree. *My* tree. Life has a way of making more sense when viewed through the branches of a tree.

Kiss me. What possessed me? I hope I never see Johnny or his brother again.

Chapter 1

I lean on my suitcase and gloomily survey Fire Station Lane. It is just as I remembered it, a stretch of grey cobblestones squeezed between a large white bungalow and the hulking red-brick of the Fire Station. There is a new hedge of fuschias, flowering in bright profusion, and a shiny ladder on the training tower behind the Station, but otherwise...

"It's like I never left." I feel depressed by the thought. Twelve years of adventures and travel have somehow brought me back to square one. And without the grandfather I adore.

"Is this the right place, miss?" The driver leans to catch my gaze. There is only one taxi driver in Mayton, his name is Bert, he has one arm and drives like a lunatic. The previous taxi driver was called Ernie. I swear you could not make this stuff up.

"Yes, my grandfather's... Um, *my* house is just down the lane, thankyou."

"Then you must be Quinn."

"You've heard of me?"

"Of course. For the record, I think you're better off without him. And it's good of you to come and help Doris."

I don't know what Bert is talking about. I look at him blankly and he opens his mouth to say something else, but then doesn't. I figure he's one of those people who doesn't know what to say to grieving relatives.

A small, hectic person in a pantsuit and purple hair hurtles up. "Bert, Bert – excuse me, hi Alfred's granddaughter – Bert take me to the train station, quick. Derryn wants me to go to the Springhill Station auction but I am *not* driving all the way out there to freeze my arse off looking at second-rate furniture and rusty farm equipment, so I need to be somewhere else, pronto."

Bert looks unhappy. "I dunno, Bill, last time I took you in my taxi I almost lost my licence."

"That was totally not my fault. You shouldn'a looked so hot in that tram conductor's hat."

"*You* shouldn'a kissed me! I nearly ran over Daisy and her cats in the street."

"Well, you don't have your conductor's hat on today so we should be hunky dory. Open Sesame, let's go." She leaps into the taxi and yells out the window, "Sorry for your loss!" as it zooms off.

Right. I decide that everyone in Mayton is nuts, grab my stuff and set off up the lane. The cool breeze tugs at my long wool jacket and my wheeled suitcase bumps along behind. It was warm this morning in Auckland, but here the wind blows straight off the mountain and it already feels like winter.

At the end of the lane is my grandfather's cottage, white with pale blue trim. It boasts an overgrown front garden, a porch festooned in wisteria and a freshly painted, weatherboard garage. My oak tree soars over all. I climb three steps to the solid little porch and try the door. It opens with a groan. Here is the cosy hall with dark timber floors, just as

I remember. Autumn sunlight filters weakly through leadlights onto faded wallpaper and an elegant hall table swathed two inches in dust.

I look up. The cornices are wreathed in cobwebs. "Thanks, Grumps, you know I hate spiders."

But Alfred is not here to laugh at me, so I drag my case over the lintel and trundle down the hall. There is his lounge room to my left, front bedroom to the right. Everything smells musty. In the lean-to kitchen at the back of the house, things look better. Here the benches are clean, a small stack of rinsed dishes by the sink. The single pantry shelf boasts a neat row of containers marked *pasta*, *rice*, *coffee*.

I pause in the doorframe and breathe. Alfred's armchair is nestled in the opposite corner by the woodstove. His small dining table lies bathed in light from the window over the sink. There is a faint smell of woodsmoke, and a draft whistling in under the back door. The kitchen cupboards, once yellow, are now eggshell blue to match the newly painted garage. Someone has been busy.

This room feels so comfortable, so familiar that I expect to see Grumps lift his ancient black kettle and say, "Welcome, Quinnie, gumboot tea? We'll have a wee natter."

But he won't. And we won't. And I don't have time for the stab of grief that slices through the butter of my conscience, because an elderly woman walks out of the bathroom and yelps, "Who are you?"

I stare at her. "Who are *you*?"

She is barely five foot tall, and bristling. "Don't be ridiculous. I live here. Get out before I call the police."

"But this is my grandfather's house! Well, it's mine now."
Being a homeowner still feels odd. Finding this woman in my
house is even more odd.

"Nonsense. Alfred's granddaughter is overseas and never
comes here." The woman looks fierce but her hands are shaking
and she leans hard on her prong-footed cane.

I feel another stab of grief. I need Grumps. Right now. I
need to ask him who the hell this woman is. He never spoke of
a woman, the executor of his estate hasn't mentioned her, and
Scarlett hasn't said a thing either.

I look again at her shaking hands and her hard, anxious
gaze. I sigh. "I *am* Grumps' granddaughter and we need to
talk." I offer my hand. "I'm Quinn Walker."

Her eyes are flinty blue, in a face that's ninety if it's a day. "I
thought you'd be taller."

"I thought my house would be empty. Can I make you a
cup of tea?"

"*I'll* make the tea." She brushes slowly past me in the hall.
"You might poison it."

It takes her ten minutes to get the heavy kettle filled and onto
the woodstove, but she looks so determined I don't offer to
help. She tells me her name is Doris Daybreak and she's lived
with Alfred for eight years.

"Doris Daybreak? That's *got* to be a stage name."

"How dare you."

Belatedly I realise that for Doris's generation, a stage career
is considered racy. Inappropriate. I switch topic. "Eight years!"

"It might be more."

"Not much more. I visited twelve years ago and I've never heard of you."

"You must have been a pipsqueak then."

"Fifteen. Pimply and full of attitude, maybe, but not a pipsqueak."

"Then it might be ten years. I'm not good at counting anniversaries." She measures tea leaves into the pot with a trembling hand and I hold my breath as she hoists the big kettle and sloshes hot water in. "I know I moved in soon after we met. Alfred didn't want to waste any time."

When my grandfather died a few weeks ago, he was seventy-six. I've never thought of him as an ardent lover. "How did you meet?"

"At the library. We were doing a computer course." She sets one mug on the table and goes slowly back for the other. "I didn't learn a thing, it was all nonsense to me, but Alfred..." Her lips tremble. "He was very kind. I'd never known a man so kind. Handsome, too."

My grandfather? Stooped with age, the way tall men often are. Bald. A little paunch. And there must have been a decade or more between them.

Doris follows my thought. "Sixteen years is no age gap when you love someone." Glory, that makes her ninety-two! She lifts her chin. "My husband of forty years was an awful man. I was glad when he died. And I never wanted children, he'd have been a dreadful father."

I look at Doris with her defiant chin, birdlike slenderness and sun-spotted hands. She seems light, translucent, like the smallest skirmish of wind might whip her away. But there is steel in her bright gaze. Her hurt has been papered over, layer by layer, but still smoulders like peat beneath. I understand suddenly how Grumps, with his kind heart and cheerful optimism, might love this fierce, broken soul.

But really. At their age?

I sip hot tea with Doris, and it is fully fifteen minutes before my predicament dawns on me. What on earth will I do now? I planned to live here for a few weeks, tidy up the place and sell it. But I can't evict an elderly lady into the street. "Ohmigod."

"Language," says Doris, automatically.

"Sorry, I just realised. This house isn't mine, it's yours!"

"If Alfred has left it to you, I won't complain."

'No, it's that common law thing, you know. If you've lived with him for more than a few years you inherit everything, just like his wife would."

"But we weren't married." Doris looks affronted. "I don't want to be married. Worst thing ever. I've *been* married and I..."

"Well, you didn't marry him, but..."

"Thank heavens."

I can't tell if she is joking or genuinely confused. "The point is, Doris, it's your house."

"No, it's yours. You said so."

I clarify. "You weren't married to Alfred, but you still inherit his house."

"I won't have it. I don't want it. How dare he impose a house on me?"

"Pardon?" I am out of my depth here.

Doris begins shuttling the mugs and the teapot one at a time to the sink. "How could I look after this house? I'm on the pension. I don't have extra funds like Alfred did, for the maintenance and rates. And I have no one to leave it to."

"You could sell the house and have the money. Rent or buy another place."

"I can't sell this house, it's Alfred's." A chink shows in her armour as she brushes away tears. "Alfred apologised on our way to the hospital... he'd never changed his Will. But he said his Quinnie will sort everything out."

"That's me. I'll sort this out."

Her chin lifts. "But I don't want his house. You're young and bright and fit, maybe a bit short for some professions, but I'm sure you can get a job and pay all the bills."

I don't bother telling her I already have a job, it's a good one and very flexible. *And in this enlightened age, no one comments on my height.* "But legally, Doris, this is your house. I have to tell the lawyer about the mistake."

"For the last time, certainly not. It's your house!"

"But where will you live?"

"I'll live here with you."

I am stunned into silence. She seems so calm, confident, adamant... And frail. I don't have the heart to tell her I'm not staying. That I want to sell the house. Mayton is *not* for me.

"What?" She is leaning on her cane, frowning.

"I'm just thinking."

"Well, don't think so loudly." She heads for the door. "I am going to bed. You can make toast if you're hungry."

I glance outside. It's still daylight. "Goodnight, Doris."

"Don't be cheeky."

"I'm not, honestly. Are you sure you don't mind me staying?"

"Alfred would expect you to stay."

"Would you like me to bring you some toast?"

"I hate eating in bed."

Feeling unsettled yet amused, I watch her painstaking progress down the hall. Apparently she sleeps in the little bedroom at the end. It's been a long day of taxis and plane travel and unexpectedly becoming housemates with a nonagenarian, and I have no idea what to do next.

I do what Doris said, and start with toast.

I find sharing a house with my nonagenarian friend is like living with a puppy. Doris sleeps like the dead until midnight, then wakes on the hour every hour until dawn. She gets up with the cockerels, makes a cup of tea, then goes back to bed to snooze. I know this because I am sleeping on a cold, lumpy couch under a thin, freezing blanket and I hear every creak in the hall, every clank of the flush chain, and the whistle of the kettle at dawn.

This woman will be the death of me.

I am drifting back into fitful sleep when Asmita calls, on her way to work. "I got your message. Why are you in Mayton? You hate the place!"

I don't need to glance at my phone to know the look she's giving me. "It's been twelve years, Az, things might have changed."

"Yeah, right."

I sigh. "Yeah. Right. I'm just here to sort out Alfred's estate and... stuff."

"The cottage you used to stay at?"

"The cottage, his clothes, his books..." I don't tell my friend I've also inherited a 92-year-old roomie who is Alfred's wife in all but name and should own my house but doesn't want it. When I flew down here yesterday, I intended to stay just a few weeks. But I have no idea how long it'll take to sort this thing with Doris.

"Don't stay too long or you'll meet some rich, dreamy farmer looking for an intelligent, well-travelled wife, settle down and never come back."

"Oo, yuck Az, is that a dream of yours? This is Mayton, it's small-town country New Zealand. No one is rich, or will admit to it, and we both know no man ever goes looking for an intelligent wife. Anyway I don't want to settle down, I never have."

"That last point is true. Why are you sorting your grandpa's stuff?"

"Because he died. It's his estate."

"Whatever." She waggles her toes at the screen, her nails freshly painted bright blue. "Why isn't your mother doing it?"

"You know how Scarlett is."

"You're such a pushover for her."

"I feel bad. She is busy with her exhibition, and I've been away for so long... Anyway, it's *my* inheritance. Scarlett is only related to Alfred by marriage, such as it was, and she doesn't want any part of it." I change the subject to chat about our mutual friends and their various partners, babies, career and travel news until Az reaches her office. I blow her a kiss. "Bye babe."

As I click off the call, I wonder how I always end up in these situations. They say life is what happens to you while you're busy making other plans. Derailed, diverted, rescheduled, that's me. Even while travelling in Europe, my plans were overset. Although I admit I did that entirely to myself, by hooking up with the wrong man.

I push aside all memories of my charismatic, beautiful and truly faithless José, and call Scarlett. I update her, and beg her for deliverance from domestic life for the foreseeable future with a step-grandma I didn't know I had. I get a riot of laughter in reply – Scarlett is amused by Alfred's romance – and a distracted, "I can't deal with that, Quinnie. I have three huge paintings left to hang and we've run out of heavy-duty hooks." I give up, get up, and go looking for breakfast.

There is no food in the pantry except days-old bread so it's toast again. I manage to coax the overnight embers to life, and put two slices on the hotplate of the woodstove.

Doris potters in, frowning. "This room should be yellow."

I add two extra slices. "It used to be, I remember."

"Did you sleep well?"

I think of the dreaded couch. "A bit cold."

"You should have used the wool blankets. They're better than the modern rubbish. What's your name again?"

"Quinn, I'm Alfred's granddaughter who..."

"Yes, yes, I know who Quinn is."

The milk in the fridge is off, but I find longlife milk in a cupboard. Sugar, too. I have an idea that sugary tea is good for shock. I think I need it this morning.

Doris surveys the cupboards. "It was that young bloke we asked to paint the garage. He *did* paint the garage, then he had some paint left so he wanted to do more jobs. Cheeky fellow. Alfred liked him, so he got him to paint the kitchen."

"Did he charge you for the extra work?" I am imagining a scam. Elder abuse.

"He didn't charge us for any work. I was *not* impressed. I told Alfred I hate being beholden to anyone."

Not a scam then. "He probably just wanted to help."

"If I wanted his help, I'd have asked for it."

"You did ask. Well, Grumps did."

"Don't argue. I could make the tea myself today but I can't stand up for long. This time English Breakfast, please." She closes her eyes. "Annoying." I am not sure whether she's referring to her fragility, the tea, or me. Perhaps all of them. "Stop wandering about. The kettle is in the servery."

I feel like I'm stuck in a time warp. "Surely you have an electric kettle?"

"Don't be ridiculous."

I locate Alfred's cast-iron kettle in the servery cupboard that connects this room with the lounge. I prop it under the tap, staring out over the back garden and wondering how I might escape the looming weeks, months and years of domestic servitude ahead.

There seems no immediate fix. After tea and buttered toast with honey, Doris parks herself with a book and I take stock of the cottage. The bathroom porcelain is stained, the hallway draped in cobwebs, the front bedroom filled with books. I feel guilt creep in over the gnaw of grief. All this dust is making me sneeze. I know Alfred was very house proud, so it seems he and Doris have not been coping. And I've been back in New Zealand for a year and not once thought to visit. Nice.

If Doris stays here, I'll need to engage a weekly cleaner, a nurse, a cook. Perhaps someone friendly to take her on outings.

Can such people be found in Mayton? Can I afford all this help without selling the house? One thing is sure, I'm not doing it all. How would I get any work done? And glory, I'd have to stay in Mayton.

First though, the kettle is whistling and Doris is hallooing. I need to make another pot of tea.

The tall, dark-haired man surveys the cottage, his eyes crinkled against the morning light. So, Alfred's granddaughter has come for her inheritance. She hasn't wasted any time. It was only a few weeks ago that the old boy's heart attack carried him off.

Johnny watches her lithe figure, her decisive movements as she shakes the rugs and hangs them on the fence, her white-blonde ponytail whipping in the breeze. *Beautiful.* A curl of attraction swirls in his belly and he crushes it. Attractive, yes, but not for him. He wonders if she is planning to live in the cottage or tidy it up and sell it.

And what about Doris?

With a grunt, Johnny sets his questions aside. So long as his peace is not disturbed, it doesn't matter what she does. He turns away and whistles for the dog.

Chapter 2

I am in the front bedroom vacuuming the ceiling when there's a thunderous knock at the door. I almost fall off the chair – another knock like that will bring the house down. Expecting a giant, I look through the bay window.

There *is* a giant, standing on the porch. Tall, with thick wavy hair, a roman profile and a grim set to his mouth. Az's prediction leaps instantly to mind but he doesn't look like a dreamy farmer. More like an oversized Heathcliff, with a swarthy dash of Mr Rochester.

He raises his hand again to the door. I haul up the sash and yell out, to stop him collapsing the house. "What?"

He meets my gaze. A lean, handsome face with fathomless midnight-blue eyes. They seem familiar, but I don't know him. His brows are strikingly arched like albatross wings. I've seen them somewhere, too.

From this angle I can see the entire left side of his face is disfigured by a vivid, angry scar. I blink. "Sorry. What do you...?"

The albatross wings meet. "I have your dog."

"Pardon?" I must have heard wrong, his voice is so deep and gravelly.

"Your dog. I've been looking after him."

"I don't have a dog!"

He looks impatient. "Alfred's dog." With a sweep of his arm he indicates the cottage and its rampant garden. "If this is yours, I presume the dog is, too?"

"I think it all belongs to Doris actually, but..." I stop. I don't need to tell this guy all my business. "Alfred had a dog?"

He scrubs one hand through his hair, and I find I am curiously attracted to this whole dishevelled, brooding look he's got going on. "He didn't talk about Clyde?"

"No."

"Doris hasn't mentioned him?"

"She has talked about Alfred, and English Breakfast tea – which she brews on a woodstove like in Medieval times, lord help us – and how short I am, and how they don't make wool blankets like they used to. But a dog? No."

"I've always thought tea was Medieval." I am unclear whether that's a joke because he immediately looks down the lane and gives a piercing whistle. There's an answering scuffle and a border collie bounds out of the bushes. Like a furry black and white torpedo he zooms up the steps and presses himself to the door with a plaintive whine.

I am horrified. "Whatever possessed Grumps to get a dog? He's *never* had a dog! And that's a young sheepdog of all things, they need so much exercise and brushing and..."

"You know about dogs?" Midnight-blue eyes fix on mine.

"I worked at a boarding kennel every weekend through college. I can't imagine why Alfred would get a..."

"Perhaps he liked the company." Is that a barb at Doris? Or me? He grunts. "The dog's alright. He has free run of the lane, and he visits me every day to play."

"You live in the lane? You knew Alfred?"

"Yes. No. Not well." He turns away.

I run round to open the front door, colliding with the dog as he bounds inside. "Whoops. Wait! I don't know your name." Inexplicably, this seems important. Something about those incredible, midnight-blue eyes. He pauses at the gate but doesn't answer. I offer, "My name is Quinn Walker."

"I know. The dog's name is Clyde." He shuts the gate and strides off down the lane.

"How odd." I stare at his retreating figure. "How rude!" The dog is running busily from room to room, so I follow him. "Don't you think that is rude? I'm new here and he's been looking after you, the least he could do is introduce himself."

I realise the dog is running a search pattern and I feel a lurch of sadness, but then he arrives in the kitchen and finds Doris. With a yip of delight, he throws himself at her, licking her face.

Doris is startled awake. "Ooh yuck, get it off me!"

I grab the dog, pushing him firmly down at my feet. "Isn't this your dog? The man said..."

"I don't know any dog. I don't like dogs. Get him away!"

I realise she is telling the truth. She dislikes dogs and she doesn't remember this one, today at least. Yet this dog clearly loves her. And it'd be odd for a bloke to deliver a dog to her door without some justification in thinking she owned it.

I stare at the dog. He curls in a ball at my feet, his brown eyes sad. "I'm sorry, Clyde, you'll have to make do with me instead." I sit on the floor beside him, feeling all the weight of my move to Mayton and the demolition of my free-spirited, city lifestyle. It is so strange being here without Grumps and his barking laugh, his chatting over tea and his bearlike hugs. Doris seems an odd substitute.

I think Clyde the collie looks as lost as I feel.

In the afternoon, the temperature drops. Wind wuthers round the chimney. I am working on my laptop at the kitchen table and the room gets so cold I can't think properly. Cursing the Mayton autumn, I go outside for firewood. Alfred usually keeps a stack on the back porch and more alongside the garage.

I am dismayed to find there's very little wood stored. "What will Doris do for winter?" The collie tugs out a hefty stick and runs off, not interested in conversation. I pile up some logs by the ancient range and ask Doris what she'd like for dinner. She says she's happy with toast. "Toast *again?*"

"With peanut butter. I'll make it." She does, and I go off to do some vacuuming. It's a little hectic because the dog insists on helping me, finding brightness in his life by chasing the vacuum nozzle around the floor. When I point it at the ceiling to suck up the cobwebs, he barks hysterically. It's a joy.

We finish in a flurry, Clyde chasing the plug back into the machine, and I put it away. He leads me to the kitchen, tail wagging, to find Doris asleep again, drooping in her chair. I wake her gently and she potters off to the bathroom then to bed. Her walls are cluttered with family photos – Doris with her parents and various elderly relatives, Doris with Alfred – professional awards, travel photos, postcards and maps. Here I see seventy years of life and work, scrawled over in her carefully looped hand. It seems Doris has achieved a PhD and a long career in agricultural science, and she loves travelling: *Went to the Riding School in Vienna, winter so the horses are stabled / Visited the Louvre and a wonderful patisserie by the Seine. / Mount Fuji is over 3,700 metres high / Close encounter with a tiger! Exhilarating!*

I ask a few questions but it is obvious Doris is tired so I leave her to sleep. I let Clyde out for a wee, and while we're in the garden Az calls me.

"How's cottage life? Are you renovating yet, and designing garden rooms?"

"I'm still here. Don't ask."

"You're back in town after twelve years, Quinn, you are an internationally renowned architect and you've just inherited a house, surely someone has popped round to welcome the prodigal daughter?"

"Not a sausage. But I'm living with a step-grandmother I didn't know I had. She is ninety-two and refuses to have an electric kettle, so we boil water on a woodfired stove." I sigh as Az erupts into laughter. "I tell you, Az, this place is so backwards. Oh, and a tall, dark stranger turned up on my doorstep yesterday and gave me a dog."

"He gave you a what?" There's a lot of noise in the background, she must be calling from the bar across the road from her office.

"Nothing very exciting, sadly." I don't know where to start explaining about Doris. Or Clyde. Az hates dogs, and there's no one in her social circle over thirty-two, including her family. She cut ties with most of them when they tried to marry her off to a distant cousin. "Look, Az, I have to go. I think I've lost the dog."

I scout around the garden and yell down the lane but I can't find Clyde. I figure that's one problem solved by itself, and head inside. The wood stove has gone out. I make a big mess of balled newspaper and flinders in my efforts to relight it, the wind whipping in through the open door to blow out the tiny flames. My toes are frozen, even in my woolly socks.

I yell again for the dog. Only the arctic wind answers. I take a broom from its hook by the door and sweep up the mess I've made. I remember the cast-iron kettle, and pour myself a lukewarm cup of tea. I scull it and feel slightly more human.

I figure the dog has had enough chances and go to shut the door, just as Clyde hurtles in. He gallops a few laps round the room and collapses by the wing-backed chair, still carrying his blasted stick. He chews it into matchsticks, right there on the rug.

"I just swept the floor!" I rummage irritably through the kitchen, lifting jars at random. "I agree with Doris, we don't want a dog. You are hyperactive and annoying and I already have enough to deal with."

I know I sound petty. None of this is the dog's fault. I feel so hungry and lost. Doris made toast and tea earlier but I forgot to feed myself. The dog is probably hungry, too. What am I doing here, playing house in this desolate country town? I thought I'd just turn up, sell the house, make some money and leave. With the Doris complexity added, I could be here for a while. And with all my cleaning and dusting and finishing the Watermill House project, I forgot to shop for food today.

I blink back tears. I am accustomed to electric heating and induction cooktops. To ordering everything online. I eat what I want, and go out when I feel like it, dancing, clubbing, shopping. I catch a bus or a plane on a whim. How can I be a free agent with this house to sort? With an elderly lady and a dog?

The dog is an unexpected problem. Should I rehome him? If I give him away, and Doris suddenly remembers she owns a dog, will she be heartbroken? Glory, I am beginning to sound responsible.

"You know we can't keep you, right?" Clyde rolls an eye at me, still chewing his kindling. "You're too young and active for Doris. And I don't want to look after you." He spits out the flinders, one at a time, with a relaxed wag of his tail. Talking to the dog breaks the silence. "There's barely any food so we've got peanut butter on toast for dinner. We'll have to go shopping in the morning." A thought nags. "If Alfred's old car will start."

It doesn't, of course. I have a fitful sleep under a couple more blankets on the cold, lumpy couch and Clyde wakes me with the birds. I let him into the garden, all my muscles aching from my terrible, makeshift bed. There is no sound from Doris's room and I can't be bothered lighting the fire to make tea. Or coffee, if there's any left. I feel a million miles from urban life, grumpy and out of place.

Scarlett is in my head. "You need meditation, Quinnie. Soothe your soul and embrace the time-honoured wisdom of stillness. Find your inner peace. Align your restless spirit to be in perfect harmony with..." I go for a run instead.

Clyde's lead training is nonexistent. He drags me left and right and into gardens, through hedges and around power poles. I run faster to distract him. It doesn't work, but feeling the burn of pure, unadulterated exercise calms my chaotic brain. With each rasping breath I am in the moment. Effort. Pain. Perfection. I pound through the cool, sparkling morning, choosing back streets at random, skirting the first stirrings of commuters and school children.

I come back depressed. Mayton is even smaller than I remembered.

I stand under a hot shower long enough to wash off the salt and my dissatisfaction. I whip on jeans and a tee and whistle for Clyde. Alfred's keys are hanging on a nail in the shed above his workbench, same as always. Apparently car theft is not a thing in Mayton. Or perhaps his Morris Minor is just so old, no self-respecting thief will be seen with it.

The Morris doesn't start. More key turning doesn't help. I unfasten the catch and lean into the engine bay. Water in the radiator, check. Oil in the engine, check. I inspect the battery to see if the electrical leads are fixed correctly, check. I think back to the pathetic sounds the car is making. "It's definitely the battery."

I sigh, step back and fall over Clyde. There is a confused scuffle and I end up on the ground, fending off his licky kisses. *Ow*. "I called you ages ago!" My jeans are scuffed, my knees grazed and stinging. I meet his hopeful gaze. "Not a hope, doggo. We're going nowhere. There's a slope on the lane but the Morris is too heavy, I can't push start it alone."

All my irritation rushes back. The supermarket is at the far end of Mayton's main street, which is rather unimaginatively called Main Street, and I don't want to have to walk all the way back with a load of groceries. I kick the front tyre. It feels so good I do it again.

"Seriously," I yell, kicking manically, "is there nothing in this house that works? I just want breakfast and a car to drive!" Clyde lolls his tongue at me and the Morris sits in sturdy silence. I think of calling Bert's taxi and reject the idea, all the eggs would come home scrambled. There is no help for it, I'll have to walk. "But you are not coming."

I find two string bags to carry my groceries, shut the collie behind the picket gate and head off down the lane. After a few seconds of hopeful whining, Clyde pops over the fence and catches up to me.

I take him back to the house and shut him in the hall. "Stay. I don't want you dragging me all over town while I try to carry things home. And don't look at me like that, emotional blackmail is a form of abuse, it means you are trying to control me." I leave again.

Behind me, the whine grows into a wail. Clyde is now throwing himself at the door. I listen to the steady thumps and wonder how long those ancient timbers will stand the strain. Worse, he might wake Doris.

Clyde is ecstatic to see me. "Did no one teach you to stay at home, you awful animal? You have serious issues." He lolls and offers me his belly. "You are a shameless manipulator." Tail wagging, he stands for his lead and I clip it on.

We set off together past the Fire Station. The tall Heathcliff-type who was at my door yesterday is rolling hoses out the back, a white tee fitted snugly over his impressive physique. He may be rude but he's also ripped and gorgeous. *Good to know.* I have a nanosecond to register surprise – *I am interested in tall, brooding men?* – before Clyde hauls me into the fuschia bushes.

I soon discover that taking Clyde shopping is exactly the bad idea I thought it would be. Our morning run has done nothing to dampen his energy. I am dragged from garden hedge to fencepost to power pole as thoroughly as though he hasn't been out for months.

It is a long, comedic adventure to reach the end of Main Street.

Thea watches with interest as the young woman and her dog make their haphazard way down the lane. On impulse, she crosses to the window with a view of the rear courtyard. Johnny is out there, checking and squaring away hoses. She slides open the sash and he looks up.

Thea tips her chin at the lane. "She looks nice." His expression freezes. "Johnny, don't tell me you haven't noticed the lovely young lady who's moved into Alfred's place?"

He puts one hose away, methodically selects another. "I took Alfred's dog to her last night."

"So you've met her?" Thea's eyes light up. "Give me the goss, who is she? What's she like?"

Beautiful. Sparkling. Like sunlight. "Her name is Quinn Walker. She's Alfred's granddaughter."

"Is she single? What does she do for work? Is she planning to sell up or stay?"

"I don't know."

Thea lifts a brow. "Johnny, you're so useless at this gig. You can't hide here forever, you've got to get out and meet people. Meet women."

"I don't."

"Bro, if you don't get better at scouting out the talent, I'll find you a woman myself."

His eyes darken. "I don't need a woman."

She gives him a long, amused look and slams the window shut. "Oh yes you do, Johnny Best," she murmurs, watching him bend to his work. "You, more than anyone I know."

It seems Clyde is accustomed to being left outside the supermarket, because to my surprise he sits quietly when I tie him to the bicycle rack.

Inside, I stock up on fresh vegetables, eggs, flour, tinned food and dog biscuits. It makes for a heavy load but I don't want toast for dinner ever again. Next door to the supermarket is a bakery sign that says Gill's Hot Buns. This is irresistible, so I go in.

Gill reminds me of the stereotypical round, cheerful farmer's wife and I chide myself for the thought. But with her striped apron, hair in a bun and a bloom in her cheeks from the ovens, Gill has stepped out of a storybook.

"A sourdough loaf and apple danish, please."

She tips her head to the side. "You're new. Are you visiting, or..?"

"I'm Alfred Cotton's granddaughter. Perhaps you knew him?"

"Oh yes, dark rye and a custard slice. I am sorry for your loss, he was a lovely man. Talked a lot about you."

"I hope it was all good."

She twinkles. "I know all the juicy bits. You like porridge with fruit for breakfast. When you were ten, you broke your wrist falling out of a tree. And about a year ago, you were jilted by your two-timing Spanish lover. See?"

"Don't remind me. José has put me off men forever."

"Never mind. You'll meet a handsome Kiwi bloke who'll sweep you off your feet."

I grin. "A rich farmer, perhaps? No, I'm just here to sort out Alfred's estate. There is nothing for me in Mayton."

"I'm sure you'll find it's not as bad as you think. Alfred lived behind the Fire Station, didn't he? Have you met Thea yet?"

"Who?"

"Thea runs the Station, with Grant and Sarah and co." Is that the trace of a blush? Maybe. Gill seems in no hurry to move on, and her assistant is serving the next customer.

"No. But a big guy knocked on my door the other night to bring Clyde home. He didn't give his name. Strong, silent type."

"That'll be Johnny Best."

I freeze like a deer in headlights. Twelve years roll back and exquisite embarrassment floods in. "That was Johnny?"

"Johnny Best, yes. I think he grew up here."

I stare at her. He certainly did. He grew huge here, acquired a deep voice, a lean, handsome face and the musculature of Michelangelo's David.

Gill is grinning. "In case you're looking, he's single."

I pull myself together. "Definitely not! Like I said, José has..."

"Oh, yeah. You have to admit Johnny has Latin Lover potential though. Just like you'd find in Europe! He's maybe not as beautiful as *before* the accident, but Sarah says..." She stops. Yes, definitely a blush.

I think of that long, disfiguring scar. "What happened?"

"Sorry, I remember now I promised not to talk about it. Sarah says it makes Johnny feel awkward." She slides my pastry into a bag and across the counter. "It's all very sad."

I stare at her. *What is sad?* I want to know everything. Who is Sarah to Johnny? Are they together? And if he got his scar from an accident, what's so bad about it that he hates people talking?

Johnny Best. I feel a strange dissonance relating that name to the dark stranger at my door. Whatever happened to the skinny Johnny Best I remember, so funny and flippant, and even shorter than me?

"Anyway, Johnny's not the romantic type. I've never seen him look twice at anyone." Gill switches topic. "Do you have Clyde with you?"

"Yes, he wouldn't stay home."

"Of course not, Alfred took him everywhere. Here's a blueberry muffin for Doris and some cheese twists, on the house. Clyde loves them."

Clyde does love them. He wolfs them down and eyes my sugar-sprinkled apple Danish.

"Certainly not, it's mine." I hook the grocery bags over my arm and untie him. "What? It's healthy. It has fruit."

To distract Clyde from my pastry, I let him drag me into the large, wooded park that extends half the length of Main Street. I hope by walking home that way we might avoid endangering cyclists and pedestrians. He is enthusiastic about the route and darts across the lawn, towing me in his wake. "Slow down, these bags are heavy!"

Clyde doesn't listen. With a whine of excitement, he plunges to the end of his lead. Clutching my bags, I'm dragged down a bank and into some rose bushes. "Clyde, wait! Stop! Jeeze, these bushes have thorns. Stop right *now* you rabid son of a..." At which point Clyde gives a huge tug, unbalancing the bags, and I fall headfirst into the carpet roses.

I roll over in the dirt and groan. There are tins of food poking into my back. Flour has exploded everywhere and I can only pray the eggs are unbroken. The tangle of thorns above me is dusted snowy white like the pale sky beyond. Forget about torn knees, I am now scratched all over, blood mingling with the flour and making a soft paste.

It's like the flour glue we made at school. An odd memory. *That crazy dog.* "Thanks, Grumps, couldn't you have kept goldfish instead?" I lie for a moment in the warm, peaty embrace of the soil. It is quiet here under the rose bushes, and my string bags are peaceful company. Then I realise I no longer have Clyde.

Panic surges. "Damn, he could be halfway home by now, or hit by a bus on the street!"

"Tranquilla, sta bene, he's fine."

"But he's so young and silly, what if he...?" Hang on.

"He is fine," the deep voice reassures me, and a large brown hand reaches into the bushes.

Chapter 3

I stare at the hand. It is the size of both my hands together. It has long, strong fingers and clean, blunt nails. My gaze travels up the attached wrist, the forearm, the beautifully muscled bicep. *Wow*.

"It's you." I frown. No wonder Clyde was so excited, he spotted his friend in the park.

There is an answering growl from Johnny Best. "Are you coming out?"

"I hope so." Annoyed that this annoying, annoyingly attractive man has found me upside down in a rose bush, I ignore his hand and wrestle with the thorns. The blasted things grip my shirt, snatch my jeans and tangle in my hair, and after a few minutes of futile struggle I give up. "Would you mind?"

Johnny grasps my waist with two strong hands and lifts me out, sets me down gently. I tilt my chin, aware of how flour pasted I am. Dishevelled. My shopping blasted all over the roses.

Those biceps, though... It was the work of a moment for Johnny to lift me. Those rose thorns barely registered. I meet his gaze defiantly. "You are Johnny Best."

"Sì."

I'd forgotten he sometimes spoke Italian. "Right. Well, then." I brush the fragments from my hair and look for Clyde. He is tethered to a bird bath in the middle of the garden, watching us and wriggling, and I feel an unexpected rush of gratitude. "Thankyou, Mr Best." What's with all this formality? I'm being weird. "For a minute there I thought I'd lost him."

"Quinn, it's nothing." A slight smile. "And call me Johnny. Only the police and my bank manager call me Mr Best."

I'd offered my hand, a kind of reflex action, and after a brief hesitation he takes it. I feel the spark of hot lightning at his touch. "Do you, er, often have dealings with the police?"

The scarred side of his mouth quirks up. "I'm a firefighter. So, yes."

"Oh. Of course." *A firefighter? Your mamma wanted you to be a doctor.* I retrieve my hand and Johnny's gaze is gone, sliding over my burst groceries.

He gestures at the mess. "Will you be alright to...?"

"Yes. It was just a silly accident and I dropped everything." I bristle at his raised eyebrow. "Clyde is a nuisance on the lead, but he insists on coming."

"Sì. Alfred took him everywhere." Johnny helps me repack my bags, minus the wasted flour. I tuck them over my arm and untie the excitable Clyde.

He asks, "Why are you walking with the dog and all this stuff? Isn't it heavy?"

"The car won't start."

"Alfred's Morris?"

"Yes. The starter motor is turning over OK, so I think it's just the battery. But I can't roll start it."

"There is a slope on the lane."

"The Morris is heavy! I can't even push it out of the garage."

"Oh." His gaze travels over my slight figure and his mouth quirks up again.

I feel a flush of heat. "It's not funny."

"I imagine it is annoying."

"Yes!" *And given the size of you, not something you'd experience.*

He says gruffly, "You know about cars?"

Men are always surprised I know something about cars. As if Alfred had been wrong to teach me. "I do. Is that a problem?"

"No. I was just wondering if you can remove the battery yourself." He shrugs. "The Fire Station has a charger. If you bring it down, we can charge it overnight."

"That'll be great!" I am beaming, standing there like a nut, and Johnny turns away. With a vague nod, he strides off down the street.

"Well!" I look at Clyde. "He is so rude, annoying, and... annoyingly *helpful*, dammit." Taking a firm grip on the excitable dog, I head back to Fire Station Lane.

The cottage feels less oppressive once the pantry and fridge are full of food. I get busy finding places for Gill's bread and my fresh fruit, herbs and vegetables, tins of tomatoes, beans, oats and chocolate. Happier now, I begin to hum. I am momentarily stumped on where to put the dog food, and eventually stuff it into a narrow cupboard by the back door.

I wedge the bag in with my foot and shove the door shut. Clyde comes panting in from the back lawn. "Bother." I open the cupboard again, pinning the bag with my foot, and measure

out two cups of biscuits. He wolfs them down, grabs the bowl
and runs off to chew that up, too.

"You look a wreck." Doris has come in.

"I had a flour explosion."

"What is that dratted animal doing here?"

"He lives here."

"Why?"

"He was Alfred's dog. Or so everyone says." And I don't
know why you don't remember him. Unless you're so
traumatised by his behaviour you've blocked him out. That I
can totally understand.

She frowns. "I don't like dogs."

"It's OK, I'll rehome him. I'll put up a notice in the
supermarket."

"You won't. If he's Alfred's dog, he belongs here."

I give up and change the subject. "Here's a muffin for you,
from Gill, at the bakery. And what would you like for dinner?
I've been food shopping so we have plenty of options."

"Toast, please."

I rebel by adding local farm eggs, poached, and creamy
hollandaise sauce.

This time when Doris settles down by the fire, I drag a
winged chair in from the lounge and sit on the other side.
Clyde curls up at my feet with a large chunk of his dinner bowl.
We watch as a gusty afternoon shower flings itself against the
windowpane, light chasing dark as the clouds scud by. Winter
is coming. Doris begins to doze. I feel a long way from my old,
sunlit apartment in Barcelona.

"Who cares?" I tell Clyde. "That means I'm also a long
way from José and his cheating ways. That can only be a good

thing, right?" He lolls at me. The comfortable, still quiet of the kitchen feels suddenly stifling and I jump up. "Come on, pestilent pup, let's go fix the Morris."

I am bent over the battery, trying to drag it out of its rusted bay when the quiet afternoon is interrupted by an earsplitting wail. In a flash, I recall Grumps hugging me close, "Cover your ears, pet. It's the one downside to living behind the Station. They call the troops with that bloody great bugle and deafen us, day or night."

I grin at Clyde. "The Station siren! I forgot. It sounds like the apocalypse."

From the Station there comes the sound of heavy boots running, and a great engine starting up. A woman's voice raps out commands over the siren's wail as it moans slowly down to silence. The lane is not quiet for long. Soon, the huge roller doors on the front of the Station rattle up and the massive red and yellow engine rolls out onto Main Street, loaded with firefighters and gear.

Clyde and I watch as the emergency lights wheel and the truck's siren whoops. The guttural diesel engine churns up through the gears. Lights flash brightly as the truck accelerates out of town.

"Pray to your doggy deities, Clyde, someone is having a bad day."

The fire truck still isn't back by the time I've got the battery out of the Morris and lugged it down the lane. There is probably someone on duty but I decide not to knock on the door. Instead, I leave the battery by the back step. I hope that when Johnny trips over it later, he'll know where it's come from. I won't forget that he hauled me out of the rose bushes today, his bronzed arms flexing, a faint smile in his eyes – but he might. He's busy saving the world, after all.

I walk home through a cloud-hazed sunset. My oak tree looms over Alfred's house and on impulse, I climb it. I go right to the top like I used to, revelling in the effort, the way my heart leaps to my throat when I look down. I have never feared heights, but perhaps Clyde does. He circles the tree, barking up at me, then lies disconsolately on the grass to wait.

I stretch out along a strong branch, my feet tucked into the trunk, my head nestled in a fork. I think about my summer holidays as a teenager in this house. Grumps' stories, his jokes, my sense of family, and feeling loved. My funny, laughing friend from across the road, who now has shuttered eyes and an angry scar. Loss, and my sense of being adrift. My grandfather was always here for me, and while I grumbled about visiting him, as most teenagers do, he was someone to hang with in the holidays and write postcards to, the third pivotal point in the tiny family triangle that is my mother, Alfred and I.

The tree moves with me, breathes with me, and I begin to calm. I can be *still* in a tree. Relaxed. It has always been that way. As a child, I would pile books and blankets into my mother's old orange tree and climb in and stay for hours. In Cyprus, I once lived in an olive tree for two weeks, recovering from a passionate liaison with an aquaculture farmer. I grin at the memory. He made very good koupepia.

That was before José. Before I was charmed – captivated? – convinced to settle down with him. Coaxed to commit. And look how *that* turned out.

Hunger at last drives me to ground level. Clyde greets me with paroxysms of delight. It is a mild night but the wind is starting to get up. The cottage is dark and cold, but I fare better this time at lighting the fire. Doris is watching TV in the loungeroom, but wanders in to help me with dinner. While I feed Clyde, this time in an old ice cream container, she starts chopping vegetables for soup. I help her with the tough-skinned pumpkin and add pasta to her big pot. I have just one cup of flour left in the exploded bag so I make a small focaccia, my fingers pressing deeply into the soft, warm dough.

I press holes into the mini loaf, sprinkle rosemary and sea salt on top, and pop it in the oven below the firebox. The kitchen soon fills with the fragrant aroma of warm bread. Time spent absorbing Mediterranean cultures while studying architecture has at least taught me how to cook. Clyde helps me to bring in firewood and joins us for dinner. He begs unashamedly for my half of the focaccia. Doris toasts her portion.

After dinner, Doris goes back to her TV program. I stare into the flames and think back to the recalcitrant Morris, and wrestling Clyde in the park. I think about Johnny Best. He lifted me from those thorns like I was a featherweight. His body is not only ripped and gorgeous but useful, it seems. Was that just this morning? It feels like a lifetime ago.

It is odd that I want to see him again. He is *so* not my type. I thought I'd struck off that friendship twelve years ago, when he and his brother embarrassed me in the street. I know I asked him to kiss me, but any 15-year-old would've done the same. He was *there* every day, running, climbing, exploring, in cahoots stealing orchard fruit with me – all the while with that gorgeous grin which lit up his whole face. Killer.

These days I prefer men with charisma and conversation. Like José, for example. Suave and sophisticated, he swept me into his crowd of acolytes and I was smitten by his erudite charm. From what I can see Johnny would have trouble finishing a sentence, let alone a conversation.

I fidget. It is Friday night and I am sitting by the fire with a dog, of all things. I am losing my edge.

Chapter 4

I suffer a third terrible night on that terrible couch and am woken at dawn by the dog and Doris. I make her a pot of English Breakfast tea, clip on Clyde's lead and go for my run. The morning is cool and overcast so I run further, climbing the hill by the cemetery west of town, enjoying the challenge.

As we walk home along the lane, I let Clyde loose so he can explore the fuschias. A tall woman waves from the back door of the Fire Station. She is striking in appearance with flaming red, curly hair. Is that Thea, the fire chief Gill mentioned? Does she live there with Johnny?

I am surprised by the twist of jealousy coming hard on the heels of that thought. I give myself a mental shake. I hardly know the guy anymore, what is he to me? I am not here to stay. If I can manage it, I'll be gone in a few weeks.

After my shower, I pull on jeans and a sweatshirt and get on with decluttering the house. The teetering piles are getting to me. Doris and I are eyeing the jumble in the third bedroom when Clyde leaps up, barking. He races out the back door and barks his way round the cottage to the front porch.

A visitor. Is it dark-haired Johnny Best, with his midnight-blue eyes?

I leave Doris browsing through Alfred's baby photos and go to the door. It is a courier guy with a parcel from my mother. He looks about sixteen, standing on the porch grinning at me while Clyde fawns at his feet.

"This place is cool. I haven't been this far down the lane before." He looks around. "Have you lived here long? Do you get lonely?" I stare at him and he shrugs. "I guess you've got all those firefighters, eh. Have you driven the fire truck? That'd be cool."

"No. Thankyou for the parcel."

"Sweet as." He slides his headphones on again and jogs back to his van.

"Really, Clyde. Even the courier guy wants our life story."

Scarlett has sent two ink drawings for me to frame and hang in my new home. Did she not listen when I told her about Doris? That I planned to sell up? I still don't know what the hell I'm going to do but I'm sure it doesn't include hanging up pictures. She's enclosed a handwritten note to explain that the drawings were by Alfred's mother, and Alfred gifted them to Scarlett when she started art classes at university.

I study the drawings. The first is of a young boy playing with a border collie much like Clyde. Rampant wisteria frames the image. Is this Grumps as a child? I look at the vines draped around my door. Here, in this garden? It appears so. His mother's sketch is a moving portrayal of boyhood and love, and perhaps explains why Alfred adopted a border collie in his later years instead of a more suitable breed.

The second drawing shows a team of horses in front of a fire station, harnessed to an engine. The scene is drawn splendidly, the three sturdy horses heavily muscled, in blinkers and chains, plunging impatiently to be off. The drawing is of *my* fire station, I realise. The one right here in Fire Station Lane.

I am still studying the drawings when there comes a loud thump on the door. Clyde erupts again in excited barking.

"Alright, alright." I walk down the hall with the fire station sketch in my hand and my head full of the past.

Johnny is at the door. I stare vaguely up at him, still thinking about vintage engines. "Oh. Hello!"

He holds up my car battery in one hand. "Charged and ready."

"The kind of service I like."

Johnny ducks his head. "Shall I stick around to see if she starts?"

"The Morris?" I nod. "OK." I set the drawing aside on the hall table, take the battery from him and lug it round to the garage. It is the work of five minutes for me to fit it into the Morris and connect it up, while Johnny stands silently in the doorway.

I slide into the driver's seat and turn the key. "Come on, old girl." The Morris gives a tentative cough, and dies.

Johnny looms at the window. "Have you checked the fluids?"

"Yes, but the battery connections are rusty, that might be the problem."

"Give me a minute." He pulls a rough cloth from his pocket and scrubs the connectors. "Try again."

I turn the key, give the Morris a little accelerator and grin widely at the satisfying rumble. "Yes! Now we're talking." I tweak the revs a little while the Morris warms up, and soon it is ticking over smoothly. I slide out of the car. Johnny seems very

near and very tall in the close confines of the garage. I smile up
at him. "Thankyou."

"You're welcome."

I am captured by his midnight gaze. *Get a grip, Quinn.* I
clear my throat. "Johnny, what do you know about the history
of the Fire Station?"

Johnny blinks at the change of topic. "A bit. It's the oldest
fire station in the district. The community passed a hat round
to raise the money to build it." His jaw tightens. "In 1866 there
was a very bad fire at a hotel in Main Street. Five people died.
After that, Mayton decided it needed a permanent fire-fighting
presence."

"What a way to get a fire station! I suppose it makes sense,
but it's horrible." I lean in to turn the Morris off, drift into the
daylight with Johnny following. "Are you paid millions to risk
your life for Mayton?"

"Not quite. Some of us are paid, like Thea and I, Sarah and
Grant. The rest volunteer for the privilege." A shrug. "That's
why the siren is so loud. It summons the rostered volunteers
from all round town in an emergency."

"They hear the siren and come running? An antiquated
system in this day and age!"

The rare flash of his smile startles me. A shadow of its
former self, but wow. "It ain't broke, so we don't fix it."

I eye Johnny speculatively. Today he looks confident in his
own skin, a little distant, interested in my conversation but not
enough to make a move. A shame.

I'm amused to find just how ready I am to forgive this
guy for not kissing me, all those years ago. I had thought it an
unpardonable offence. On reflection, I give myself some credit.

He *is* tall, dark and handsome, and while he's *not* a stranger he has a mysterious past and an intriguing scar. It's perfectly reasonable to look twice at a man like that.

Johnny has never known what to do with Quinn. Well, not since that summer night when... Then he knew absolutely, but he wasn't brave enough to do it. At the Fire Station he is surrounded by mechanically-minded and capable women, but Quinn... He hasn't seen her for a decade, he'd convinced himself she would never return, and now she *is* back – as bold, bright and beautiful as ever. He is utterly, impossibly attracted to her. It *is* impossible.

With something like alarm, he hears himself say, "If you're interested in the history of the Station, come and talk to Thea. She likes that stuff too. She's gone home already today, but she's rostered on tomorrow."

"Great! I will." Quinn's eyes are hazel, shot with gold. They glow when she is enthused. Johnny has to look away. Too much of that and he'll be in big trouble. Again. He does not deserve attention from a woman like her, he will not seek it.

"Right, then." He walks away.

"OK." I check with Clyde. "Was I boring? Did I say something offensive?" I think of that beautiful roman profile, those biceps and the tamped down, simmering heat in those dark eyes. "Mm, a shame."

But now the Morris is driveable so I can get on with some jobs. I want to buy new bedsheets so I can get off the couch, and storage boxes for Alfred's stuff. I will also take the two drawings to be framed.

"Come on, Clyde, let's go into town. We'll avoid rose beds this time." I pop my head round the door to let Doris know, and I clip on Clyde's lead. We jump into the Morris and I try the key. The vintage, inline four-cylinder starts like a charm.

I can't keep from smiling as I ease the little saloon car out of the garage and down the lane. "Grumps, this is a gorgeous car. I forgive you for the spiders and the flat battery."

Clyde gets plenty of practice on his lead down Main Street. I stop first at the lawyer's office, there is only one in town, to ask for an appointment. The reception desk is empty so Hemi comes out in person to greet me. He is a burly man with a smiling face, a large pounamu greenstone pendant and warm, brown eyes. I tell him he looks too friendly to be a lawyer.

"I promise to destroy you later. Financially, that is." He grins. "I will send you an enormous bill to restore your faith in the degeneracy of my profession."

"Perfect." I decide I like him. I ask about an appointment and he tells me four weeks. "Four weeks!" Perhaps I don't like him after all.

"I am sorry, but there's only me here and a lot of legal work."

"Enough to keep you that busy? How many criminals can a little town have?"

He laughs. "Not just criminal law. I deal with employment law, business contracts, land disputes, Wills, divorces, custody arrangements, you name it. If I can't do the work myself, I refer clients to specialist lawyers elsewhere."

I wish *I* was elsewhere. But I think Doris should come to the appointment with me, so I book with Hemi for four weeks' time.

Clyde charms the staff at the homewares store and steals biscuits from the ladies at Little Bird Bookshop. I call in at Little Bird because Clyde drags me in the door, and while I am untangling myself among the bookshelves I notice a sign that says 'Picture framing'. The proprietor, Olive, is ecstatic to meet Clyde and even more enthusiastic about my art pieces.

Olive studies the drawings intently, her silver hair electric. "These are stunning, just *look* at those horses. Kate, come and see!"

Kate is serving coffee at the window. Her green eyes study me with interest. "You must be new here."

"Yes, I've moved into my grandfather's house."

"Where is that?"

"In Fire Station Lane."

"A nice place. Tucked away, but central. Have you met any locals yet?"

"Just Gill at the bakery. A courier kid. And one of the firefighters helped me out of the rose bushes in the park."

She grins. "There's a story I'd like to hear. A firefighter to the rescue!"

Olive waves the drawings. "Never mind firefighters, Kate, come and see these horses. I'm sure this is drawn from life, the artist has paid incredible attention. Look, the fire engine is so detailed, and the harness is accurate."

I feel a rush of pride for my family's artistic skills, and gratitude my mother sent me the artworks. Perhaps they belong in Fire Station Lane. Immediately after this comes the discomforting question of what I will do with them when the house is sold. I try to ignore it.

Kate bends her honey-blonde head. "The drawing of the little boy is so sweet. And Linc will like this one with the horses."

"No doubt," says a deep, warm voice and a lean, handsome man slides onto a stool at the coffee bar.

Kate's eyes sparkle and she leans to kiss him lingeringly. "Hello, my love. We are admiring some drawings that Quinn brought in. She has moved into the little villa behind the Fire Station. Quinn, this is the love of my life, Lincoln Brady."

"That's me." Linc reaches over to shake my hand. "Welcome to Mayton, Quinn. I was sorry to hear old Alfred passed away, he was a good bloke."

"Thankyou."

"I reckon I've heard about you." His gaze is amused. "Weren't you in Vienna a while back? Alfred showed me your postcard of the Lipizzaner horses."

"Yes." I grimace. "I think everybody's heard of me and my postcards."

"It's sweet, we all get our turn in the gossip column round here." He glances sideways at Kate.

She laughs, flicking a teatowel at him. "That's not fair, I didn't gossip about you!"

Linc's dark eyes are teasing. "No. You just drew all kinds of conclusions from minimal data."

I raise an eyebrow and she blushes. "It's true, Quinn. For a while, I thought he was married to his sister."

I laugh, and Olive tut-tuts, pushing between us to place the horse sketch in front of Linc. "Never mind that, Lincoln, look here. Do you think we can date this drawing from the harness? I'm guessing late 18th century, perhaps early 1900's."

"It's a good drawing. Yep, it's hard to date it from the horses' harness but they're pulling a steam-powered water pump, so that puts it after 1870. They ran manual pumps and handcarts here prior to that." He takes the sketch from Olive for a better look. "It's interesting that there are three horses. In the few historical photographs I've seen, the local engines were drawn by two." He returns the picture with a smile. "They're good-looking horses. Not Clydesdales. Dark points, finer feather."

"Yes, and with very little white on their faces." Olive frowns. "Some other heavy breed, or a solid crossbreed. They put me in mind of the Belgian draught."

"In New Zealand? Unlikely. They're probably bred from the Suffolk Punch horses imported around then, along with Shires and Clydies."

As Olive and Linc launch into an animated discussion about the merits of various draught horse breeds, Kate smiles at me. "Coffee? These two could be a while."

"Yes, please. Flat white with one sugar."

She heads for the coffee machine. "How is Doris? It must be hard for her, losing Alfred."

"It's hard to know. She seems very stoic. I imagine she is really sad but she doesn't show it. And she's got me running around brewing tea every five minutes... To be honest, I think Doris lives mostly in the moment."

"Perhaps it's not a bad way to be when you've lost a loved one." Kate hands me the coffee and gives Clyde a pat. "I see you've inherited Alfred's dog."

"Yes. He is certainly not Doris's. She doesn't remember they had a dog! I take him out and about so he doesn't bother her."

"Is he the reason you ended up in the rose bushes?"

I laugh, "How did you guess?"

Her eyes twinkle. "Clyde used to tow Alfred all over town, and I can't imagine he has reformed in just a few weeks. He's a menace to traffic but we love him."

"I'm trying to train him on the lead but he's so young and reactive, it's difficult."

"Tell you what, let's swap numbers. If you end up in the rose bushes again, or need anything at all, ring me. I've only been here a year so I know what it's like to be new."

"Thanks, though I don't think I'll be here long, this place is too dull for me."

Kate chokes on her coffee. "Too dull? Maybe on the surface... Personally, I find Mayton hugely entertaining. Come and make coffee here at Little Bird for a day, you'll find it very educational."

"I just don't think I can stay in a town this small. After living in Europe, Mayton feels like the middle of nowhere."

"It is!" She grins. "I grew up in London, and I lived in Sydney for a while so I know what you mean. I didn't think I'd stay either, but then I met Linc. We have an amazing life together here."

I look at Lincoln. He is conversing intensely with Olive, a smile lurking in his gaze. He senses us watching and casts a sly, unhurried wink at Kate. He is one gorgeous package, I can see why she stayed.

I leave with another coffee in hand and extra biscuits for Clyde. I am confident Olive will do a good job of framing the drawings, she's been so complimentary of them. "Kate met Linc right here in Mayton," I tell the collie as we drive home. "It's obvious he adores her! I didn't believe men like that existed."

My thoughts slide unaccountably to a certain tall, dark firefighter. I don't mention him to Clyde. I have a feeling that if Clyde learns I want to use Johnny for his body then just leave town, he won't approve.

Chapter 5

As usual, Clyde and Doris wake me at dawn. I pour tea for Doris, make coffee for me, and let Clyde out to run in the garden. "What would you like to do today, Doris?"

"I don't have any plans. I'd like to read the second novel of this author I'm reading, but I have no idea where to find it."

"The sequel?"

"No, the first book. The one I'm reading. I can't find it anywhere."

I help Doris find her book, then go looking for the sequel. Because it's probably in the piles of books in the front bedroom, I am motivated to declutter.

I collect Alfred's personal papers and stack them for sorting with Doris. While I'm working, I chat with Az. I tell her about the pictures Scarlett sent, and she tells me about work and her friends, and teases me about becoming way too domesticated down here in Mayton. She thinks an intervention is needed. Clyde is wreaking havoc with my piles of paperwork so I hang up, feeling that our conversation was somehow discordant and dissatisfying.

I pack the important papers into boxes. Then I box the books in the front room. I put all the books Doris wants into her room, and keep a couple for me. The rest go into boxes to be given away. There are some old hockey sticks and a dusty aquarium, which I carry to the garage. I will eventually have to get rid of Alfred's clothes but I won't bother Doris with that yet. I leave Grumps' macintosh hanging on its peg by the back door, it doesn't seem right to move it.

In the smallest bedroom, I find teetering stacks of vinyl records. These are surprisingly diverse in genre, albums from the 1950's through to the 90's. I decide these need more time and thought, so I pick out a couple at random and close the door on the rest. At least I can see enough floorboards and walls now to give the cottage a thorough clean.

There is a record player in the front lounge. "Do you mind, Doris?"

She is daydreaming over her murder mystery, and puts the book aside. "Of course not. Alfred loved that thing." I slide Electric Light Orchestra's Out of the Blue from its tissue sleeve and set it to play. Doris conducts the music while I dance round the room with the mop, randomly sloshing water and enjoying the hell out of myself for the first time in days.

Clyde chases the mop around, getting muddy prints everywhere until I grab him and turn him outside. I exchange my mop for sugar soap and get busy scrubbing the walls. It is several hours before I realise Clyde hasn't come back in. I switch off the record player and whistle for the dog.

There is no answering skitter of paws or snuffling from the bushes.

Not again. "Clyde!" I bellow. Still nothing. "Damn." I exchange my ugg boots for sneakers, pull on Alfred's macintosh and do a tour of the garden. No dog.

I look down the lane, feeling rising panic. Why panic? Damn, I hate this dog. What if he's run off down Main Street? What if he's been hit by a car? I vault over the gate, sprint down the lane past the stationyard and run straight into Johnny Best.

I rebound with a yelp, and he catches me with both hands. "*Ay*, what the...?" I clutch my stomach. "Seriously, who needs a Mack truck when you are around?"

"I'm sorry." Johnny's hands are still at my waist. He snatches them away. "Sorry, Quinn. Are you alright?"

"I'll live." There is a tingling in my body where his hands touched me. All over, in fact. Does he feel it, too? No, he looks much like he always does. Uptight. Indifferent. "I'm looking for..."

"Clyde, I know. I was coming to tell you. He's watching TV in Thea's office."

"Really?"

"He likes the dog food ads."

I can't tell if he's being funny or serious. I decide on the latter. "I had a heart attack when I couldn't find him."

"If you lose him, check at the Station first. He hangs out with us most days. He'd go home when Alfred called him for tea."

"Oh." I blink back sudden tears at this snapshot of Clyde's life.

Johnny makes a quick move towards me, then stops. "Please don't cry. Clyde is happy with you, I see it. You take good care of him." I smile at him. Glory, I need to toughen up. He clears his throat. "This might not be a good time, but you could come and meet Thea?"

I scrub my face with my baggy jacket sleeve. I have cobwebs in my hair and I am dressed like a tramp. "How about I finish cleaning, then come down in about an hour? Will Thea still be there?"

"Yes. We're rostered on until eight."

"Cool." I skip backwards, wave, and run home to the villa.

As Quinn dances away, a whisper of loss settles over Johnny like a cloak. He flinches. He doesn't need more loss and heartbreak, more beautiful people in his life who can get hurt, or leave him, or both. Better to stay as he is, with the simplest life possible and a minimum of risk and pain.

He gives a half-smile. What is a firefighter's life *but* risk and potential for pain? But this is different. He can handle pain in the body. It is pain in the heart which almost killed him. He never wants to feel that again.

Quinn turns up an hour later in new jeans and a loose silk shirt, her hair brushing her shoulders. To Johnny, she sparkles, and his heart lifts at the sight of her. He has been changing tyres in the workshop to distract himself from watching for her, listening for the slam of her front door, but it's useless. He hears Clyde's whine at the yard door, Thea's warm greeting, and his attention is caught. He puts away the wheel brace and socket and heads for the tea-room.

Thea and Quinn are already chatting passionately over the Station's collection of photographs when Johnny walks in. Thea meets his gaze over the top of Quinn's head. 'This woman,' she silently telegraphs, 'is The One for You. I know it.'

He rolls his eyes and crosses to the hot water urn. "Tea, anyone? Coffee?"

I hadn't seen him come in. I glance up. "Coffee, thanks. Milk, one sugar." For a moment our gazes catch, and it's an effort to drag my attention back to Thea. I'm behaving like I'm 15 again. "Do you still have the horse-drawn engine, Thea? I'd love to see it."

"We sure do. We hold onto everything around here. Even when we'd be better making a fresh start." Thea looks pointedly at Johnny, but I'm lost as to her meaning. "Give us a week or two to determine what we have in storage, then I'll give you a tour."

Johnny sets two coffees on the table. "That's Thea Bramley code for, 'Give us a week or two so Johnny can clean up all the old engines.'"

"That's why we love you," she grins, reaching for her mug. "Mm, that's good, ta." She tilts her head at me. "Men. You've just got to keep 'em busy."

"Amen to that. The last man I left idle while I worked long hours found time to run off with our rich neighbour."

Thea throws back her head and laughs. "You see, Johnny? There can be no rest for you. We can't let you run off to another fire station, no matter what they offer." She leans in conspiratorially. "Johnny is our best driver. There is no place on earth he can't take a fire engine. So, you see we cannot lose him."

Amen to that. I watch Johnny as he shrugs self-effacingly and turns back to the kitchen. I can't see much of the Johnny

Best I knew, but I am drawn to his quiet strength, the ripple of muscle under his shirt and that dark, dark gaze. Already I know life in Fire Station Lane would not be the same without Johnny Best.

Thea turns a page in her album and exclaims, "That's a very early photo! Look, there's the steam-powered water pump we were talking about, with the horses to pull it – and by that shed at the back is a handcart." She frowns. "I didn't know we had a photo of a handcart."

"They really pulled that clunky thing around town by hand?"

"Oh yes, the earliest fire equipment was handcarts, with manual water pumps mounted on top. And bucket chains, of course."

"Hard work."

"Very. The buildings were all made of timber, and people used flames for lighting and heating, so every household kept buckets of water ready in case of fire."

I study the photograph. There is bunting draped above the horses' heads. The foreground is blurry, but it looks like the people are standing around a big cake. "Is it a party of some kind?"

"Oh yes, the Station has a commemorative fête every five years. It's a longstanding Mayton tradition. The next one is in five weeks' time. We've begun the advertising, and Gill will make the cake, but I need some ideas, you know? I'd like to do something a bit different."

I feel a tickle of interest. "You mean you want some kind of feature event?"

"I want something different to our usual – you know, visits with the fire truck to local school fêtes, squirting the teachers and kids with water. A fresh idea, something big."

"Something big. Something different... How about a display of the old fire equipment? Or... a parade?"

Thea whoops. "A parade! Hear that, Johnny? You can drive the truck in a parade."

I ignore his frown. "You'll need more trucks, though. You can't have a procession of one. What happens to your old fire trucks when they're decommissioned?"

"They get auctioned off. Great idea! We can ask the owners of our old trucks to bring them on parade. The ambulance and police will probably join us, too."

I wave the photograph. "Could you get a replica handcart built? Like this one?"

Thea points at me. "Yes! Let's do that, too. Johnny, find someone to build me a handcart. I'll pay for it myself if I must."

Johnny borrows the photo from me. "It looks simple enough. I'll ask Dave if he can make one."

"It must look just like that one. There may be regional differences in the designs, because in that era the handcarts would've been built locally."

"All good, Thea, I can do it."

I am still thinking about the parade. "How about getting horses to pull the steam pump?"

"Whoa..." Thea stares. "That would be so cool. I wonder, Johnny..."

He shrugs. "It might be possible. Linc knows about that stuff."

I look up. "Kate's fella?"

Thea is amused. "Quinn, you can't imagine. It was the biggest upset in Mayton this century. Hearts were broken all over the place when Linc fell for Kate Dale. He was the most eligible bachelor in town, but once Kate turned up he had eyes for no one else."

"Love at first sight?"

"Just about. Linc is a quiet bloke but we could tell he liked her."

"I met them yesterday at the bookshop. They seem very happy."

"I think Kate is perfect for him. They're great together."

Johnny clears his throat, gruffly. "Anyway, Linc knows about harness horses so we can ask him."

Thea looks startled. "The harness! I hadn't thought of that. The steam pump is still in pretty good nick but the harness is probably ruined. It hasn't been cleaned or oiled for years."

"I'll ask Linc to check it."

I am still buzzing. "You could have the whole history of fire equipment on show! You can get schoolkids to carry some buckets like a bucket chain, then the handcart can come trundling along..."

"Then the horse-drawn steam pump, and any vintage trucks we can get hold of, and Johnny's truck. Fantastic!" Thea looks up as a young woman walks into the room. "Sarah! This is Quinn. Grab a pen and paper and sketch her ideas for the Commemoration – the parade, the decorations, everything. I have to go make a call."

Sarah takes Thea's place at the table and I go through everything with her. "Thea says you already have a cake organised. Can you decorate it to look like the Fire Station?

You know, brick walls, a roller door on the front, maybe a fire truck inside..."

"I'll ask Gill."

"Gill with the Hot Buns?"

"That's her." Sarah looks a little pink. I file Gill's name under Possible Romantic Connection.

I begin scribbling notes. "About the local community. If you can get school children involved, you could design some learning activities around the Commemoration, like the art classes my Mum used to do. Bring the kids here on a visit, and ask the schools to decorate some buckets for the parade. You could show students the old photos, tell them stories about firefighting... Do you still have a library in town? They could do a display and book readings."

"I reckon Lollie would love that. I'll show her the album tomorrow."

"Vintage recipes, maybe high tea and scones. Invite the whole town, your local councillors, a few politicians from Wellington – who knows, you might end up with more funding. And can you find someone to cater for, say, an afternoon tea?"

"Gill might like to cater. I'll draft the invitations, and Grant can write them. He has beautiful calligraphy."

"You need to get the word out pronto, to find those old engines Thea was talking about. They could be sitting unused in barns, or converted to campers..."

Sarah busily scribbles her list. "Word out. Newspaper... social media... design a flyer, put it on the noticeboard outside the stock feed shop..."

"And you want this all done in five weeks? Mamma mia."
Johnny escapes to make more coffee.

I nibble the end of my pen. "A photographer. You need
someone who can take really nice photos."

"We'll ask Sue. She does all the event photography around
here."

"And you need decorations for the front of the Station, you
know, bunting and flags."

Thea is back, leaning over Sarah's chair. "Great idea! Can
you do that, Quinn?"

"Me?"

"Sure. Order what you think is best and we'll cover the
cost. Johnny can get the big ladder and help you put them up."

The thought of getting up close with Johnny on a ladder is
attractive, but I have other plans. "Sorry Thea, I think I'll have
left Mayton by then. I'm just here to sort out the estate." And
put the house on the market. And rehome Doris and Clyde.

For someone who has umpteen volunteers at her beck and
call, Thea looks more disappointed than I'd expect. "All good.
Thanks for the ideas, anyway. If you are still here in five weeks,
I'll put you to work!"

Chapter 6

On my way out, I am still buzzing from the impromptu creative session we've had, and excited about meeting Thea. I look up to see a young woman in a wheelchair coming down the lane from my house. "Hello!" This seems to be my day for meeting people.

"I'm Lollie." She sticks out her hand, smiling, her bushy hair flame-bright. "You must be Quinn."

"Not you, too."

"Oh yes, Alfred talked about you nonstop. I've just been up to drop a casserole in for Doris. Don't thank me, it's the least I can do, I live right here." She opens a side gate leading to the white bungalow on the corner of Fire Station Lane and Main Street. "This is our house. We get a front row view every time the fire truck goes out."

I follow her in. "What a glorious car!"

Lollie strikes an extravagant pose in front of her Mini Countryman. "Ta da!" It is striped red-and-white like a candy cane, with a yellow roof-rack for Lollie's wheels. "Meet Milly Molly Mandy."

"Gorgeous! You must feel like a circus troupe driving around in that. Why did you paint it Milly Molly Mandy colours?"

"I collect old children's picture books. I *love* them. I inflict them on all the children who come to our book-reading sessions at the library. And yes, I probably look like a circus, but it's *fun*."

And that, I decide, sums up Lollie perfectly. I tell her about the idea of putting Mayton's fire-fighting history on display in a parade, and Lollie is soon bubbling over with ideas for book readings and archived records she can show the school students.

We make an arrangement to meet at Lollie's tomorrow for coffee, and I go home to think of a new way to serve toast. This time I will ladle a rich beef casserole over it.

Lollie's house is open and light, her shelves stocked with picture books and vintage toys. The corridors in her home are extra wide and the kitchen benches low to accommodate her wheels.

"You have a lovely house." I spin in circles under the skylight in her kitchen, watching her dreamcatchers twinkling. The house has a warm, bright feeling.

"Thankyou. Adam is a builder so we did the renovations ourselves."

"Handy."

"Yes. And sexy! There's nothing sexier than a man working in your kitchen with power tools."

I laugh. "There's nothing sexier than a man working in your kitchen, fullstop."

Lollie nearly drops her coffeepot. "My dear, I believe we'll get on famously."

While Lollie pours from her colourful ceramic pot, I browse the shelves. "The Railway Children! Oh, and look at your Asterix & Obelix collection. The Faraway Tree! I'd forgotten all about it. Alfred read the Faraway Tree to me one Christmas."

"Borrow anything you like. Just make sure you return it or I'll have to murder you one dark and stormy night. I can't help it, it's the librarian in me."

"A fine excuse for murder."

"Any decent, well-read judge will understand." Lollie looks down at her wheel. "No, Clyde." He stops gnawing on it and rests his head in her lap. She strokes his ears. "How is he going without Alfred?"

"I think he's a bit confused. He seems happy enough, but at night he still goes round looking for him."

"That must be hard. You must miss him, too."

"Growing up, I had only Alfred and my mum, so he was like a father to me. If Scarlett was preparing for an exhibition, she'd send me down here to stay with him. Now I feel bad that I stayed away for so long."

Lollie points a scarlet fingernail. "No guilt allowed! Alfred *loved* that you lived in Europe. He showed me all your postcards and dined out on your adventures for years."

"It's just that... I hadn't really thought about him getting old."

"Alfred was OK. He had Doris, they were very happy together. We live close by, and there's Thea and her team. When Johnny came to live at the Station, he started going round to help with odd jobs." She ruffles Clyde's silky fur. "Of course, Alfred also had his dog!"

"And what a dog it is." I throw Clyde a complicated look. He dragged me through a gorse bush on our run this morning so I am feeling particularly ambivalent. "Did you say Johnny lives at the Station?"

"You know Johnny?"

"Kind of."

"Yes, Thea lets him stay there. Sort of like a sexy flatmate and caretaker all in one." Lollie sparkles. "I wouldn't mind Johnny as a flatmate, he is drop dead gorgeous... But Adam says three will be a crowd."

"Inconsiderate of him."

"I thought so." She pours me another coffee, and we talk about my career designing high-end homes for wealthy British and American families, and her career enthusing people in Mayton to read books. "And how are you getting on with Doris?"

I don't know quite how to answer that. We are getting along well, just as long as I don't play anything too modern on the record player, anything past about 1980, and I keep making toast and tea on a regular basis. Doris has now relinquished all responsibility for making tea, perhaps because the old kettle is so heavy. Lollie laughs when I explain that Doris won't let me buy an electric one.

"But I am going to install a new TV so Doris can watch her favourite programs on demand. I don't think she will object to that. I think she finds it hard to read at night – some problem with the light, or perhaps her eyes." I ruffle Clyde's ears. "To be honest, Doris feels like a big responsibility. One I didn't expect. Until I arrived at the cottage last week, I didn't even know she existed!"

Lollie's gaze is kind. "And now you have a readymade family of step-grandma and collie dog, and no idea what to do about them. Will you sell up, rehome your step-grandma and the dog, and go... Or stay in Mayton and do... what?"

"Ugh, it's a dilemma which goes round and round in my head every night." When I'm not thinking about our resident firefighting Michelangelo's David. "I don't want to stay in Mayton! But every day, I see more reasons why Doris needs me, or at least someone *like* me to... I don't know, be here. Help out. Care."

"That's nice of you."

"Not my usual state. I'm hoping this is a phase."

"You know she has wonderful neighbours like me." Lollie bats her eyelashes.

"It's not really the same. I worry about her bringing the firewood in on her own, or going out to the garage to hang the washing. There are so many things she insists on doing herself but she's really quite frail..."

"I understand. What does Doris want to happen?"

"She wants to keep Alfred's house because, well, it's his. She wants to live in it with me, while I own the house and pay all its costs."

"And you don't want to do that."

"No. Technically the house should be hers. And I had plans to sell it." Had? Since when did this plan slide into past tense?

"I have to tell you, Quinn, when I visited Doris today she looked more relaxed than I've seen her since Alfred died. A few weeks ago she was in a terrible state, forgetting things, dropping things, I was really worried about her." Lollie glances at the cuckoo clock on her wall. "Heavens, I'm due at work in fifteen minutes! I'm sorry, Quinn, I've completely forgotten the time. I need to dash."

"Can you drop Clyde and I down the street? We want to look at televisions."

"TV's? The Evans family run an electronics store just along from the art gallery. Try there, I'll tell them to give you a good deal."

"Perfect."

Within a few minutes Clyde, Lollie and I are strapped into Milly Molly Mandy and tootling down Main Street. I have never seen hand controls used before, so I am intrigued.

Lollie is happy to show off her car. "I go easy on speed bumps because she's so low to the ground, but what she lacks in height she makes up for in enthusiasm." We turn off the main street and roar along Candle Road to the cemetery. "See? Here's second gear, third, fourth..." She pulls up to demonstrate neutral, then slams the car into reverse and whizzes backwards all the way to Main Street.

"Lollie!" I nearly choke laughing.

"It's OK." We hurtle through the intersection and she makes a wheel-skittering turn fit for a rally driver. "There's only one policeman in town and he's married to my sister." She pulls over sedately. "Your turn. Jump out, we'll swap seats."

It takes me just a few minutes to learn how to use the hand controls. By the time we get to the electronics store, I'm in love with Milly Molly Mandy and Clyde is getting car sick.

I toss him out to retch in the street while Lollie swings back into the driver's seat. "That was a riot. Next time, bring Doris with you for coffee!"

"I will. But not for coffee. You'll have to dust off your teapot."

She laughs and zooms away, now fully half an hour late for work. Clyde seems to take a while to recover. He is unusually well behaved, looking at the TV's, and only wraps me around one tree and a street sign on the way home.

Chapter 7

It is all Clyde the Collie's fault. If he'd stayed inside the fence, I wouldn't have chased him over the fence and then Johnny wouldn't have driven through it.

I've never seen the fire truck this close. It is usually parked out front in the workshop, hunched like a bear ready to boost through its doors and lumber to the rescue. I've had no cause to worry about it. And as far as I can tell, my old paling fence has been unmolested by it for ever.

This morning, as I sit in my tree, I hear the *beep beep* of a truck reversing up the lane. Looking down through the leaves I see the flash of hazard lights, the vast bulk of the fire truck moving towards me. It dwarfs the wind-tossed fuschia border, the timber fences either side. It even dwarfs my house. My tree, though, towers above all. I love this tree. It is the best thing about Alfred's cottage.

Down below, Clyde the Collie is a black and white whirlwind. He is chasing autumn leaves, most of them blowing down from my oak. Like a furry cork he bobs from the front lawn to the back, swirls under the clothesline and eddies round the shed. Soon he is drawn to the front again, twirling by the picket gate and washing up on the steps of the vine-encrusted porch. Here he pauses, tongue lolling.

He spots the truck. In the brief time I've known him, I've learned Clyde is not prone to caution. I yell, "Clyde, no!" as he rockets towards the fence.

The palings are unkempt and Clyde knows the gaps. He flows through the fence like water. The fire truck is close now, beginning a careful manoeuvre out of the rear stationyard, its great haunches swinging left, the warning *beep beep* sounding incessantly. I begin a desperate scramble down the tree, see the wing mirror of the truck come round, the raven hair and dark eyes of the driver reflected in it.

Johnny Best. He, of all the fire fighters, must not run over the collie dog. He, of all the fire fighters can probably best avoid it. Without further thought, I throw myself over the fence and under the truck to grab Clyde.

That my fence is the only casualty is a miracle, really. But after the truck has veered wildly, the hiss of air brakes has subsided and Johnny has climbed out through the rhododendrons, he doesn't look much like a hero. He looks more like the Incredible Hulk. A Hulk in a towering rage.

"*Oddio!* What did you do, jumping under my truck? Do you know you could have been killed?" Johnny has an Italian mamma and in moments of crisis it shows.

I laugh, my arms full of wriggling, furry dog. "That was incredible! I can't believe you missed the garage, I thought it was a goner."

Johnny's eyes flare. "*You* were nearly a goner! It is lucky that I missed you. And Clyde, what if I'd killed him? Mamma *mia.*"

I feel that his reaction is excessive. Clyde does dumb stuff all the time. Me, too, but perhaps Johnny doesn't remember that. I release the dog, transfixed by how hot this man looks, how *alive*, those lean albatross wings arched over a gaze alight with anger. Fear.

I recall my manners. "I am sorry. I was in the tree so I couldn't catch him in time."

He pauses, the lift of an elegant wing. "In the tree? Why?"

"I like trees." This brings a sudden, flashing smile from him, the one he used to have. I look into those midnight eyes and say without thinking, "Kiss me."

His gaze sweeps the cobbled lane, the dog at our feet. "Here?"

My heart is pounding. There is a roaring in my ears. "Yes, here. In Fire Station Lane."

Johnny looks hard at me. Then he slides one hand behind my head, strong fingers laced in my hair. We are close, I am barely breathing. Our eyes meet, mine dancing, his with an edge like a knife. He leans in, his mouth meets mine and he kisses me, long and slow.

I am laughing, sure he won't do it. My laugh slides into a surprised burble and becomes a rolling, satisfied noise deep in my throat. I reach up to touch his face, the sandpaper scrape of his jaw. Johnny deepens the kiss and my edges dissolve. I am as weak as a kitten, weightless, breathless. I lean into that hard, strong body, hot lightning streaking through every point we touch.

Clyde the Collie whines, from somewhere at our feet. Johnny blinks. Gently, he releases my mouth. His arm is still wrapped round me, our noses touching.

"Ay *ay*." My breath comes on a sigh. His arm is a solid bar supporting me, his hand entangled in my hair. I am not sure I can stand up. "Now *that's* a kiss."

"You asked." Humour flickers in his dark blue eyes and I feel the rumble of his voice where our bodies meet.

"Mm." I did, and not for the first time. *What was I thinking?* I get my feet back under me, and he releases me. This close, I am reminded how tall Johnny is. Huge, broad-shouldered, a giant about the size of his fire truck.

That reminds me of something else. I look across at the hole in my fence, his truck parked inside it. "Can I ask you to fix this, too?" But Johnny is already walking away, his head down and his stride long. He disappears around the stationyard wall.

I look down at the dog and straighten my dress. "Don't be so judgemental, Clyde. I just wanted him to unbend a bit, he's so..." Uptight. Annoying. Good at kissing.

I stare after Johnny. Really, really good at kissing.

Leaning against his truck, my heart still pounding, I decide that I should think very carefully before asking him to do anything like that again. Johnny Best... Who'd have thought? My spirited, carefree, single existence may not survive another kiss like that.

Skirting the shattered palings, I head back to my tree. I don't feel up to seeing Doris, I need a moment to breathe. A tangle of familiar branches and russet oak leaves is just the place. I'll never admit it, but being that close to the fire truck was terrifying. Amid the squeal of tortured brakes and tyres, I thought Clyde and I were both goners. Never mind the garage.

I'm lucky Johnny is as good at driving as he is at kissing.

———— ⟨∾⟩ ————

That Kiss leaves me good for nothing. After lunch with Doris – tomato bruschetta – I find a Georgette Heyer novel in Alfred's piles and take it back to my tree. I am daydreaming about this firefighter – his mouth, at least – like a lovelorn teen. Glory, Johnny can kiss. I remind myself I hardly know him. This man is a different beast to the Boy Next Door of my summer holiday memories. Bigger. More sombre. With a shuttered gaze and that beautiful, baritone voice that gets me right in the... I smack myself awake with my book.

All this dreaming. What for? Another time, another place I'd jump into bed with him, get it over with, and move on to live in an olive tree. I am losing my edge.

Sarah comes over to collect the fire truck. She waves to me in my tree. I devour *The Quiet Gentleman* whole and come down when it is too dark to read. Clyde escorts me in a happy flurry into the house.

It is time to make toast. This time with creamy mushroom soup. How did this become my life?

I really need to get a bed. This couch is a demon's curse. I drag myself out at first light and jog blearily down the lane. With Clyde skittering on the pavement beside me, I soon settle into a steady pace. The wide street is adrift in autumn leaves and thin tendrils of mist. It is so early, Olive's coffee window is not yet open. Most of the shops are shuttered.

As we pass Gill's Hot Buns, the scent of fresh baking wafts out. I miss a step and Clyde veers enquiringly. "No buns. We are running." I jump over Clyde's lead while he does a few loops, and find my stride again. "Don't give me that look. Maybe later."

We pass the memorial park and the hardware store. Here, Main Street makes a slow curve to the north-east and dips gently to meet the river. There is a picturesque bridge in sight, spanning wide brown water, and a panorama of willows, bush and farmland.

Coming across that bridge is a sight that stops me in my tracks. I stare in awe, as Clyde surges forward, barking. "Clyde, no yelling."

Two horses are coming over the bridge, their hooves clattering on the timbers. They are pulling a beautiful carriage, their harness clinking, dawn light glinting off the brass lanterns and paintwork. Two people sit high in the front seat, in comfortable conversation, the man driving his horses with a light, steady hand, the woman in a Victorian-style dress and bonnet.

I crouch at the edge of the road, put a calming hand on the dog. "Clyde, sit."

The carriage rumbles past the bridgehead and the horses lean into their collars, trotting up the rise into town. When they've crested the hill, the driver says, 'Whoa' and the horses slow to a stop. They look very big, this close. I can feel their warm breath as they snort and champ their bits.

"Ciao!" I exclaim.

"Good morning, Quinn." Kate is beaming, her colour high, her hair dusted with dew. She has her hand tucked through Linc's arm and he nods. "Morning."

"This is amazing. You guys look amazing! The horses, the little brass lamps, everything. Kate, what a gorgeous costume, you look like you've stepped out of a story."

Linc grins. "I hope it's Kate's story. I hear Lady Hatwick's coachman gets plenty of..." Kate stamps hard on his foot.

"You've written a book?"

She looks flustered. "Yes. No. It's just gone to print."

"If you want to read it, Olive will have it in her shop next week." Linc ignores the elbow in his ribs.

"That's so cool, Kate!"

"Thankyou." She seems keen to change the topic. "I must say it *is* lovely this morning. Worth all the bother of getting up early."

"What bother?" Linc is still smiling. "*I* got the horses in before dawn, brushed them, harnessed them, I even brought the carriage round. All you had to do was..."

"Climb three steps in button boots and a full-length skirt. *And* I made a thermos of coffee!"

"That's some serious effort right there," I agree.

"I stand corrected. I'm happy to slave for years if Kate will make me coffee." He kisses the top of her head. "Anyway Quinn Walker, all this fuss and bother is your fault."

"Mine?"

"Yes. We are out here getting the horses fit so they can pull that enormous fire engine of yours for the Commemoration."

"The Station's birthday?" I can't believe it. "But Thea said..."

"I know, but after she rang the other day I went round and had a good look at the old Station harness. It needs some work but I reckon I can jimmy something together."

"Linc is great at working with leather." Kate looks proud.

"That will be awesome!" I jump up in excitement, setting Clyde dancing round me. "To see the horse-drawn fire engine out and about like this will be incredible. Thankyou, Linc. Wow."

His brow furrows. "I don't think we can get the steam pump working in time, though. Johnny knows some guys in the Hutt Valley who restore steam locomotives and they said they'll take a look at it, but for the parade we'll at least be able to pull it down the street. The shafts are in good condition and Johnny will make sure the metal fittings are safe." Linc gives the reins a brief twitch. "What do you reckon, Dash, want to be a fire station horse for a day?"

"She's got the right name for the job." I look at the horses, one red, one grey. The grey horse rubs his bridle against the red one's face and gets a sideways nip for his trouble. "Which is Dash?"

"Dash is the chestnut mare. The grey is Waiata."

"When we met, I'd only just moved into Waiata Homestead," says Kate. "Linc was training the grey horse, and for months he had no name. One day I suggested 'Waiata' might do."

"Mm," purrs Linc, and Kate treads hard on his foot.

"It's a good name. He is as pretty as a song." I step out of the horses' path. "I'd better let you get on."

"I think we've interrupted your run. Would you like a ride home?" Linc tips his chin towards town. "We're going down Main Street anyway."

I want to say yes, but then I remember Clyde. "Will your horses be happy carrying a dog?"

Kate laughs. "We have my sister's rowdy twins onboard, I'm sure they'll cope with the dog!" She looks round and calls, "Boys!"

There is silence from inside the carriage. She frowns, glancing at Linc. "Do you think they've jumped out?"

"Probably." He grins. "Hopefully while we were going over the bridge. They can starfish down to the estuary and Hemi will catch them in his whitebait net."

Kate gives him a Look, then sings out, "Taika, Nikau, speak up or *no* hot chocolates at Olive's!"

There is a burst of raucous laughter from inside the carriage. It lurches as two little boys lean out of the window, shouting, "Auntie Kate, we played a twick on you!"

"Yinc, we played a twick!"

He is smiling. "You are horrible, obnoxious little children who deserve to walk home."

"We is not walking."

"Yuck."

"We want hot chocyate."

"Yum. Hot chocyate."

Kate waves a hand. "This is our friend Quinn. She is going to ride with us. Her dog, too."

Linc explains, "Kate's nephews, Taika and Nikau. I'm afraid there is no excuse for them. Jump in. Use the folding step. You lift the door handle to open it."

I pull down the ornate little step and bundle myself and Clyde into the carriage. The little boys embrace the collie in delight. He wriggles up beside them on the bench seat and presses his nose to the glass.

I tap imperiously on the roof. "Drive on, sir!"

"Go, Yinc!"

"Yay, we going. Yook, yady Quinn, we going!"

Johnny feels a flicker of surprise when Quinn turns up in the landau. He had not thought Linc Brady was the type to... but then he sees Kate on the box, and he feels the tension flow out of him. Quinn opens the door and two little boys and the collie dog tumble out ahead of her.

Clyde has enjoyed his ride and jumps up to tell Johnny all about it. "Down, boy."

"Yay, Fireman Johnny!"

"Hayyo, Fireman Johnny, we riding in da yando!"

"Morning Taika, Nikau, good to see you." Johnny hugs them as they buffet into his legs, then they hurtle off after the dog.

"Doggy, come wiv me."

"No, me!"

From the raised seat, Linc nods at Johnny. Quinn barrels into his space, crackling with energy, collecting Johnny inside her forcefield of joy. "'Morning, Johnny! Aren't the horses beautiful? Linc says you are helping him to fix the old fire engine. Down, Clyde, stop jumping."

Kate smiles at him. "We met on the bridge. We are getting the horses fit, they've had a very lazy summer." She claps her hands to get attention. "Come on, boys, let's go to Olive's for hot chocolate!"

"Yay, hot chocyate! Me first!"

"No, me!"

The boys abandon the dog and pile back into the carriage. Kate climbs up beside Linc and the horses move off.

Quinn watches as the landau rumbles down the road, its little lanterns swinging. She looks wistful, standing there in her running shorts with a bandaid on one knee. "Imagine travelling by horse and carriage everywhere. That'd be so cool."

Johnny thinks it would be monumentally inefficient, but he doesn't say so. He just soaks up Quinn's halo of energy, letting it seep into the cracks in his soul. She is mercurial, magnetic, irresistible. He can't look at her mouth without wanting to kiss her. Again.

He frowns. Especially when she is standing in front of him in those tiny, cute shorts, showing all that midriff.

He mutters something incoherent and walks away.

I turn from watching the landau to discover that Johnny has gone. "Clyde, you are a useless sheepdog. Next time, keep him here. Bite him if you have to."

I'd planned to invite Johnny to breakfast. I'm thinking if I can get near him for more than two minutes at a time, I might actually get to know him. And Doris won't mind looking at him over her toast. I want to get a grip on who he is as a person, as a friend – not just some boy I once wanted to kiss.

Still want to kiss.

I nibble at my lip. That stuff has never bothered me before.

Chapter 8

Thea arrives at work full of plans for the Commemoration. She calls Johnny into her office to go over logistics like the catering options, staffing allocations, the things the council will require to approve a temporary road closure for the parade.

Johnny ends up with a big list. It includes collecting some signs that Thea has designed to advertise the event. "Easy, I will visit Mamma this afternoon and pick them up on the way home."

At Johnny's mention of his mother, Thea looks away. She doesn't want to embarrass him, but she'd do anything to take away that lost look in his eyes. She closes her laptop with a snap. "Take my car. It has more room to carry the signs."

Neither says it aloud but they both know Johnny does not have a car. At least, not one that he will drive. When his mamma moved to the Hutt Valley to live with her sister, Johnny moved into the Fire Station. Their family house across the road stands empty, Mario's boots still at the door, his jacket in the hall.

About once a week, Johnny rides his motorcycle over the hill to see his mamma at Rosa's small, boutique hotel. Today he takes Thea's car and is greeted effusively when he ducks under the vine-draped doorway.

"Ciao, tesoro," Rosa exclaims. "You are not on two wheels today? I am pleased." She bears him up the stairs on a wave of kisses and commentary about his mamma's health, her dietary peculiarities, and anything of note she has said since his last visit.

Mamma is sitting in her corner bedroom, staring out the windows and rock, rock, rocking on her creaky old chair. If she notices Johnny, she shows no sign of it.

"Ciao, Mamma." He leans in to kiss her on each cheek.

Today Rosa has more worry than usual crammed into her dark eyes. "Our Giulia, she is weak today, *amore*, I worry."

"I will ring the doctor and ask her for a home visit." Johnny leaves to bring in an armful of groceries from the car, then looks again at his mother. He cannot see any perceptible change in her expression but she is no longer rocking the chair.

His aunt tells Johnny of a water pipe that is leaking, so he goes downstairs to fix it. Rosa often asks him to fix taps in the café or bar, or change light bulbs in the hotel rooms. He works diligently, his head down, a little piece of his heart still in that corner room, crushed under the creaking chair.

When it is time to go, he kisses his mother. "Ti voglio bene, Mamma." *I love you. I can't fix you. Mario is gone and cannot return to us.* He leaves by the back stairs, avoiding Rosa. Back in Thea's car he hunches in his seat, staring hard for a long, miserable moment at the ivy-clad hotel wall. Rosa's gate is not hung properly, he notices. He will bring tools next time to fix it.

Eventually, he gets on his phone to the medical centre and arranges the doctor's visit. Rosa appears at a window and waves at him. He nods, and she kisses her fingers, *Ciao, tesoro*. What else is there to do? He starts the car, recalling Thea's instruction to collect the signs from the workshop.

The young design apprentice flirts outrageously with him. Johnny can't help but smile as he fields her invitation to the cinema then, failing that, the next music night at Rosa's bar. *Mamma mia*, he can imagine Rosa's litany of questions if he arrived with the apprentice in tow. Is she a good girl? Who is her family? Look at her dyed hair, doesn't she realise that shade of green looks terrible with her complexion? Declining her invitation is a mercy for the young woman.

Johnny hunches deeper into his jacket, slides the last of the signs into the bed of the wagon and shuts the door. Thea's car is heavier, more cumbersome through the hills than Mario's '72 De Tomaso Pantera would be, but definitely more practical. And there's no way those signs would fit on the bike. He feels the tug of a grin. Yep, you could always trust Mario to choose looks and speed over utility. And it had to be Italian, of course.

He feels a twinge of guilt. He is unsure now if the Pantera will even run, he's left it so long in the shed. That red beast of a car was so much a part of Mario, so expensive, beautiful and outrageous, that when he died Johnny closed the garage door and blocked the Pantera from his mind. He feels sadness creeping in. It is not the car's fault that Mario is gone.

This thought takes him to a dark place, so he veers towards happier thoughts. He thinks of Quinn and the old Morris Minor she's inherited, her quick, sure hands as she reconnected the battery the other day, her teeth biting her lip as she frowned in concentration. She could barely reach the battery terminals, but he'd known better than to offer to help.

He is sure Quinn would like the Pantera. She radiates something of its heat and spark.

Thea is out when he gets back. Sarah helps to unload the signs and stack them in the tea-room. Grant makes coffee, and the three of them sit around shooting the breeze until Thea turns up.

"What are you lot doing sitting here? Remember we have a training day tomorrow. Have you cleaned out the tower? All that firewood has to go." Johnny jumps to his feet as Sarah and Grant groan, they'd forgotten all about it. "And here's the good news, Johnny. All the wood we have left was intended for Alfred, so you can deliver it to Doris and the lovely Quinn."

Now it's Johnny's turn to roll his eyes. Sarah looks at Thea's grin, then back at Johnny. Her blue eyes widen. "The lovely Quinn? Ooh la la, tell me, have I missed something?"

I am in my tree recovering from a bruising session teaching Doris to use her new TV when a shadow crosses the lawn, then another. Soon after comes the squeal of wheels and the deafening clatter of firewood tumbling onto our back porch.

Thea halloos up to me. "Afternoon, Quinn, how's the view from up there? I'm putting my guys to work in the community today, more specifically your backyard."

"Oh? Does our garden look that terrible?" I climb down to meet her. I like Thea, there is something irrepressible about her.

"We store firewood at the Station every year and let it dry. Then we donate it to all the old timers. It's a community service, a bit of a gym workout, and it keeps the guys happy."

Thea twinkles at me. "Alfred was one of our old timers. You are his family, so we're bringing his firewood for you."

I feel a wash of gratitude. "Thankyou!" Over Thea's shoulder, I see Johnny and two more fire fighters pushing empty wheelbarrows back down the lane to the stationyard. "I guess this explains why Alfred and Doris don't have firewood stored for winter. They knew you would turn up with it."

"Always." Thea looks at me. "Please don't cry. Your grandfather was a big supporter of the Station, and we supported him right back. That's how things work here."

I scrub at my face. "I'm not crying."

She grins. "Look, I'm still busy with our list for the Commemoration but I think these guys need supervising. There's a lot of firewood and if they don't stack it properly you'll be tripping over it all winter. Do me a favour, Quinn, and tell Johnny how things should go."

Is that a twinkle in Thea's eye? I stare after her as she strides past her team and down the lane. The wheelbarrows are soon back at my gate.

"Hi, Quinn." It is Johnny. Can you fall in love with a voice? "This is Grant, and this is Sarah." The firefighters reach to shake my hand. I am conscious of Grant's tanned, blonde bulk and Sarah's friendly brown eyes but I can't focus on anything with Johnny so close.

"Hi Grant, Sarah, thankyou for the firewood." I want to breathe Johnny in. Gaze at him all day.

"We left the first load in the porch. It won't all fit, though. Do you have room in the potting shed?"

"Yes. No. Do I have a potting shed?"

Johnny's smile quirks. "Behind the garage."

"Really? Clyde should have told me." I wrench my eyes from the tall, handsome man in my garden and dart off down the garden path. This is ridiculous. I need to get some distance so I can think properly. I jog round the house and there it is behind the garage, a little shed I've never noticed before, unkempt and covered in ivy.

I haul open the narrow door. The interior is gloomy, filled with garden pots and rusty tools. I inspect the walls and low ceiling for leaks. The floor is lined with neat rows of old bricks. It appears dry, and once cleared out it will be perfect for firewood.

Johnny comes to look. "See? Potting shed."

"I see." I can feel heat rolling off his body. I gaze at the rolled sleeve of his uniform, his forearm inches from mine as he leans on the doorframe. "Nice."

Johnny lifts an eyebrow. "It's pretty messy actually, but I could help you clear it."

"Yep, that's exactly what I meant. Totally. Let's get started."

Back at the front gate, Sarah grins. "What do you reckon? Smitten?"

"Smitten," Grant grunts. Sarah whoops and high-fives him.

"Nonsense," Johnny growls. "For that, you two can clean the wheelbarrows."

"Worth it." Sarah spins her barrow with a flourish and leads the men back to the Station.

I can't stand the thought of another quiet night fireside with the collie. Things are moving so slowly with Johnny – *is* it even a thing? – and I am so up and down I feel the need to shake things up. Go out. Listen to music. See people, dance, drink, make a noise.

From my morning run I recall a streetfront café advertising a regular Blues Club on Fridays. I decide to go and check it out.

I hit the shower, style my hair into waves, and unfurl a mid-length sleeveless midi dress from my suitcase. It is shimmering champagne satin with a generous side slit, and thankfully won't need ironing. I hate ironing. Once I've paired it with matching strappy heels and gold hoop earrings, I feel ready for anything. I shut Clyde in the kitchen, grab my black wool jacket and head out the door. This time of night Doris is in bed and Clyde is happy to laze by the fire, so no one complains.

The Fire Station looms as I trip past in my heels. I take care walking on the slick cobbles and I'm grateful for the warmth of my jacket. A single bulb burns on the back porch of the Station and subdued lighting washes from the truck bay.

I hear the bass riff reverberating down the street well before I reach the café, and just as I am beginning to regret the strappy heels. The door is shut tight against the cool night air but a neon sign says 'Open'. The band is doing full justice to T-Bone Walker's *Stormy Monday*. I pause on the step to tidy my hair and am nearly bowled over by a guy coming out.

"Whoah." He grabs the door to stop it swinging back and looks me over appreciatively. He is mid-fifties maybe, solidly built, carrying a chrome cymbal stand. "You must be new here."

"It shows?"

"Oh yeah. I haven't seen a dress like that in Mayton since Hemi and Rae's wedding." He pauses meditatively. "Actually, not even then."

"Now you're making me nervous." I tip my chin at the door. "Am I over-dressed?"

"Honey, they'll love you." He sticks out his hand. "I'm Ira. Gimme a minute to fix this and I'll come in with you, if you like."

I trail after Ira to his nearby van. It has 'Electrician' written on the side, so I make a mental note in case Doris and I need anything done at the cottage. I watch as he rummages for the right-sized nut and washer. He can't find them so he wraps the stand with black electrical tape and slides it up and down a few times to be sure it works.

"You play drums?"

"When my kit works. Dave's filling in while I sort this. He's usually on the blues harp but he can play a bit of everything." Ira opens the café door and the music swells. With a flamboyant bow, he ushers me inside.

"Quinn Walker!" Lollie's bellow cuts clean through *Sunshine of Your Love* and every head turns. "You look sizzling, babe!"

I go with it and squeal, "Lollie!" She hurtles up to me, tips back her chair and spins, the fairy lights on her wheels winking like gold gems all over her red skirt and my champagne satin.

Ira is grinning. "I see you and Lollie have met."

"Ira, you're a doll but she's mine now. Come on Quinn, I'll introduce you." Ira heads for the stage and I follow Lollie to the tables by the dance floor. "This is Mel, that's her hubby Dave up there on drums. This is Morrie, Vaughan, Mira, Christa."

I nod to everyone and get friendly smiles in return. "Kate's busy putting the raffle basket together so we'll catch up with her later. Over here is Billie Carlisle. She and her sisters run a couple of shops on Main Street. Tell me, Quinn, do you like dancing?"

I throw off my coat and wiggle. "In this dress, do you have to ask?"

"True babe, it's a given. Billie, you coming?"

A woman with purple hair, the one who ran off with Bert and my taxi, beams at Lollie. "I'm all yours, girlfriend."

By now Ira is back on drums and Dave launches into the wailing harmonica intro for *The Boys Light Up*. Billie grabs my hand and a fistful of Lollie's scarf and we bop onto the dancefloor together. Lollie tips and spins and Billie twirls me round and round, and soon I forget my angst and restlessness, lost in the laughter and the music.

Perfect. This is perfect. I'm beginning to think there might be some good in this sleepy, two horse town.

Johnny takes his bike for a spin to clear his head after work. Riding home along Main Street, he sees Café Diva is lit up. Friday night. He'd forgotten. It'll be good to kill some time. He parks his Harley against the gutter, kicks out the stand and wedges his helmet on the pillion rest. He is tired. Bone tired. It has been a long day.

His mouth quirks. Except for a brief highlight this morning, taking firewood to Quinn. That potting shed was a complete surprise to her. He always feels so slow around that woman, it was nice to be ahead of her for once.

He steps into the warm wash of music and Diva's Friday night vibe. There is Linc on bass and Ira on drums driving *Every Little Thing She Does Is Magic*. Hemi is working his own magic at the microphone. There is Christa at the bar, Mira clinking glasses with her, Billie and Lollie hotly engaged in haggling for raffle tickets with Kate Dale. He considers going over to help, but it seems like Kate is holding her own. There is Morrie calling for the band to play *Wagon Wheel*. There is...

Ah. What a dress. What a *woman*. A sparkling, white-blonde sunbeam in the middle of the dancefloor. It's a pity she is dancing with Brad Evans. Johnny sucks in air, rubs a hand across his jaw, turns to leave. He thought an evening at Diva would relax him, but he hasn't considered the Brad factor. The Quinn factor. The Brad and Quinn...

Hang on. Quinn isn't looking so good.

Dick Trelaney is behind the bar, and Johnny catches his eye. "How much has Quinn had to drink?"

"Alfred's rellie? I dunno, I swapped out with George for a bit. But she started on tequila shots with Billie half an hour ago and you know how that ends up."

"Yeah, I know." Johnny's jaw tightens. He watches Quinn spin and stumble a little, sees how tight Brad is holding her. Perhaps to keep her upright? He wonders if he should intervene. Probably not. She's travelled the world, so most likely she can handle herself. From up on stage, Linc catches Johnny's eye. He tips his chin at Brad and Quinn and raises an enquiring brow.

Johnny shrugs. He knows there is no love lost between Linc and Brad. But he also knows why. So he stays in the shadows, watching the dancefloor. Deep inside, a small voice whispers that he is going too far. Delivering firewood for Quinn is quite enough, he doesn't need to watch over her like this.

Johnny ignores the voice. Too much of the rest of him says otherwise.

When the song changes, Brad steers his dance partner to the bar, Johnny's gaze still on them. Quinn seems lost in the music, singing to herself, but when Brad offers her a shot glass she shakes her head. "No more. I just want... dancing."

"Come on. Jus' a liddle... One more." Brad is three sheets to the wind himself, and clearly wants to crack on.

"No!" Quinn wags her finger in Brad's face. "Dancing."

"Jus' one."

"Dancing." She flicks her wrist expertly to release his grip and sashays back to the band. As Brad makes a move to follow her, Johnny slides between them.

"*Bella*, dance with me?" The sheer bulk of Johnny brings Brad up short and his face falls, comically.

"Johnny!" Her hazel eyes glow. "*Claro*. Oops, sorry, that's Spanish." She confides to Brad, "He brought me wood today." She leans into Johnny. "Johnny Best. Did you know you are really, really..." She tilts forward and he puts a steadying hand at her hip, "...really tall?"

"That is because you are very short." Johnny's heart is in his throat, he never does stuff like this. He slides his hand up to meet the curve of her waist and steers her onto the dancefloor. The band has read the mood and slowed the tempo. Rae is up now, singing ballads.

Quinn laughs. "Not nice thing to say... to a lady."

Back at the bar, Brad waves his empty glass. "Cheersh, Trelaney, fill 'er up!"

Trelaney sighs and reaches across to take it. "You've had enough, mate." Brad bickers briefly, but the barman knows his job.

Brad gives up and slumps on his stool, glowering blurrily at the dancefloor. "I didn't know Johnny Besht could waltsh."

"Mate, none of us did."

I leave when the band starts packing up and my long walk down Main Street is sobering. That, and the blister starting on my heel.

As I limp homewards, I think about dancing with Johnny. His touch was tender and attentive and I was surprised how lightly he danced. Dancing is essential to me, just like air, and food, and trees. Dancing with that guy in the silver shirt was a chore. With Johnny, it felt like breathing. Smooth. Easy. Even a little tipsy like I am.

I take off my shoes and carry them slung in one hand. There is no traffic tonight but a single, loud motorcycle, and as I've climbed into someone's garden to pick flowers I don't actually see it go by.

I am climbing back out over the garden fence when I meet Johnny. He has his helmet tucked under his arm and he's walking fast. "Oh. You ride?"

He pulls up short when he sees me, seems instantly to relax. "Yes."

I hitch my skirt off the fence and look into his dark eyes. "And you dance. You kiss. You drive a fire truck. It seems to me you're good at everything." I yield to tequila-fuelled impulse and press my hand to his chest. There's a tight black tee under that leather jacket, stretched over hard muscle. Glory, he feels good. "You know what, Johnny? I want to know what *else* you're really, really good at."

His mouth quirks. "You've been in Mel and Dave's garden."

"You can tell?"

"The tiara is a giveaway."

I pause. "I asked you a question."

"I'm not going to answer it."

"That's not very polite."

"Gentleman's privilege."

"Nuts." I adjust my flowers so I can see him properly. "Is this Mel's garden? Do you think she'll mind? I met Mel tonight. And I think Ira was playing Dave's drums. Oops, no, other way around." We walk a few houses further and turn into Fire Station Lane, the mossy cobbles cold under my feet. "I just picked lobelias and alyssum, there was so much there."

"I don't think Mel and Dave will mind." He cleared his throat. "My... brother and I stole from their garden all the time."

"I can't imagine you stealing anything." I raise a finger. "Oh wait. We used to steal apples, remember?"

"Your idea, every time. I went along to keep you out of trouble else Mamma would box my ears."

I laugh through my wilting lobelias. "I'd like to see your mama again. And your brother."

I notice he goes quiet, but that's pretty usual for Johnny. I hum a few bars of the band's final song, lift my fingers to frame the oak tree in my garden and peer through them.

When Quinn mentions his brother, Johnny's heart thumps hard in his chest. *You can't see him. But he would've liked you a lot. Perhaps too much.* Mario was handsome, confident and a daredevil. He could talk better than Johnny, dance better, and definitely thought he could drive better.

It is Johnny's considered opinion that Mario and Quinn would hit it off like firecrackers. *If Mario were here, right about now I reckon I'd be standing alone in the dust of the red Pantera.*

I fish for my house key. "Come in for a drink?"

He ducks his head. "Not tonight."

I pout. But I am mellowing, blissed out on music, dancing and flowers, and the night is cold. "Goodnight, Johnny Best."

Johnny's eyes are hooded in the dark. "'Notte, bella."

Chapter 9

The Morris needs a drive to keep its battery topped up, so in the morning I go round to Little Bird Bookshop to check up on my drawings. Olive has framed them beautifully in textured black frames. They are double matted, antique white on top, grey at the bottom, and far too stylish for Alfred's cottage in its present state. I know that if I put in the effort, I could make a home worthy of them.

"But I'm not sure I can be bothered, you know? I'm clearing out the clutter because it annoys me, but I'm not one for settling down. Even if Doris wants me to stay."

Olive sympathises. "I was the same at your age. Perhaps I still am. I live in a tiny house with my huskies and a cat. Not all together, the huskies live outside. But I might move on again one day." She shakes out her electric hair. "Mayton has a pull, though. It has its own gravity. You get to know the people, you fall in love, you stay."

"I have to fall in love to stay here?"

"There are all kinds of love." Olive is packing my pictures into a box with a little bird logo on it. "I was hopelessly in love with a tree, once."

"I fall in love with trees all the time! My soulmate is a big, old oak."

"The oak in Alfred's garden, at the end of Fire Station Lane? That is the most beautiful oak in town. You have very good taste in trees, Quinn."

We grin at each other and I take my package, ready to leave. "Oh, I nearly forgot. Do you have any copies of Kate's book?"

"I do, they came in this morning. I was just about to put them on display." Olive dives into a box and pulls out a paperback with a bright pink cover. "Do you read romances?"

"I read pretty much anything." I study the illustration. A buxom woman in Regency dress, two plunging carriage horses and a dishevelled coachman. "This looks like fun."

"I must say Kate is a dark horse. She was such a shy thing when she first turned up, wouldn't say boo to a goose. And all the while she was typing away about this Lady Hatwick character getting it off – or on, or something – with all these fellows in every grand country house in England."

"*Ay*, I can't wait to read it."

Olive twinkles. "Kate nearly died when I said I wanted to stock it, but I know it'll be a bestseller."

I drive home in the Morris with my drawings and my book, and take Lady Hatwick up the oak tree for an hour before lunch.

The night has always been to Lady Hatwick like water is to sport fishermen, essential, energising. Dressed in her finery, roaming the corridors, she realises she has never understood her country friends' penchant for early bedtime. Fortunately, the young earl staying in the east wing feels the same.

"My lady." He turns from the window, his shapely silhouette partially illumed by the glow at the end of his cigar.

"My goodness," she murmurs. *If it had been the elderly Duke smoking by the window, she'd have been forced to take evasive action. For this gentleman, however...* "I find I cannot sleep. Perhaps it is the moonlight through my shutters. A little... exercise may be beneficial. Will you take a turn with me, my lord?"

Lord Silk makes an elegant leg. "At your service, my lady."

"How very fortunate."

I come down from my tree, chuckling. "I could tell you all about it, Clyde, but it'll make your fur stand on end."

I am fed up with sleeping on the couch. Over lunch I consult with Doris, and we decide to tidy the big front bedroom and move me in there.

"It was Alfred's library," she says. "Having a library made him feel posh. But he doesn't need it anymore."

"I'll need to buy a new bed. I'm not moving that horrible couch in."

"You can have the bed from the vinyl room."

"You mean the room full of old records?"

Her love for Alfred shows in her smile. "He kept buying them and putting them away. He said one day people will want records again, not those shiny, temperamental disc things."

"CD's."

"Yes, those."

I don't have the heart to tell her CD's have gone out now and digital streaming is in. But Grumps was right, vinyl records are back in vogue. Doris seems pragmatic, not gloomy, about me taking over his library so I get started.

I move all the shelves out, sugar soap the walls and mop the floor. I discover the bed Doris mentioned, buried under the teetering records – it's very big, the largest bed in the house crammed into the smallest room. I move all the records off, dismantle it and drag it round to my new bedroom. The mattress is the hardest to move.

I haul the mattress round the bend in the hall, puffing and heaving. "Seriously, where is a man when you need one? You find them lining up when there's dancing to be done, or kissing, but when I need help to move furniture..."

Doris is sympathetic. "Men! They're only good for one thing."

Clyde is running back and forth on the mattress like he's running on the backs of sheep. I growl at him, "You seem to think this is fun. If you had opposable thumbs, I'd be putting you to work."

My housemate waves her cane triumphantly. "You can't put *me* to work."

"Any more cheek like that and I'll think of something for you to do!" It is a novelty, laughing and bantering with Doris. When she smiles her whole face lights up.

I rebuild the bed near the bay window and dress it in new bedlinen. I plump up the pillows and bring in a bedside table, a fringed lamp and Kate's book. I open my suitcase and unpack my clothes into the wardrobe. The curtains are dusty and torn so I hang a couple of my embroidered manton shawls in the window instead.

While Clyde cavorts about, entangling himself in the discarded curtains, I admire my handiwork. "Don't tell my mother, Clyde, but this looks almost domesticated." I pause, looking at the two framed ink drawings. I've stacked them by the wall for now, and Alfred the little boy smiles at me. He is so happy playing with his dog.

I gaze at him for a long time. I feel I've eased into some kind of rhythm here, living in my grandfather's cottage, but I have no idea what I'm doing long-term. Delayed. Derailed. Domesticated.

I turn the pictures to the wall.

Doris makes her inspection before dinner. She pats the bedspread and admires the shawls. I give her a blue one for her room and suggest, "Dinner time?"

"I think we should eat less carbohydrates. I saw it on TV. Less pasta, less rice."

"Toast is out, then?"

"Oh no, I'm sure sourdough toast is acceptable."

In the evening, I stand under the streetlight at the end of the lane while Clyde snuffles through the fuschia bushes. I can't help it, my eyes stray to the Fire Station. Light spills from the windows and makes a thin, bright line under the workshop doors. I pick a leaf from the nearest bush and roll it in my fingers. Somewhere, Johnny is playing cards with the team on standby, doing paperwork, or reading propped against the wall on a cot in the back room.

I let myself imagine he is thinking of me. *Please, please, just for a moment*. Like I am thinking of him. Of the way his hair curls over his collar, blue-black in the light. Of his beautiful olive skin, the strong line of his jaw, and his midnight-blue eyes. Of his hands, and the way they would feel if he...

I drop the leaf. This will never work. Johnny is not thinking of me. He will never come to me like that. He is too quiet, too reserved, and I am not going to ask. Look where that got me last time.

Well, the time *before* that.

I head for my porch. "Clyde, come!" The collie comes running. "Good boy." Instead of thinking about Johnny, I will climb into my newly-built bed and read about Lady Hatwick's erotic adventures.

Johnny turns into Fire Station Lane just as Quinn calls the dog. Clyde erupts from a nearby fuschia bush, lolls his tongue laughingly at Johnny and dashes up the lane to the cottage. Johnny stands in the shadow between street-light and Station, watching as darkness swallows the dog. He imagines Quinn bending to greet the collie in her garden, reaching with her small, quick hands and giving her quick smile to say, *Well done, dog* and *I love you.*

He blinks. Where did that come from? No one will say *I love you* to him. Who could? He failed his brother. He does not deserve love, or even the hope of it.

Johnny rubs his face in exhaustion, rolls his shoulders. He's walked for an hour along the back streets of Mayton, round and round this little town, and not figured out any answers or felt one iota better. But just one look at that happy, laughing dog, one thought of that gorgeous, sexy, powerhouse woman and he feels hope sliding traitorously under his skin. Lust, pulsing deep in the pit of his stomach. Love, gently unfurling where it has no business to be.

He has to admit it. He feels peace. Johnny doesn't want to be anywhere other than Fire Station Lane. Because Quinn is here, too.

I finish Kate's novel in the wee hours of the night and lie back on the pillows, chuckling quietly. Who would suspect that quiet, gentle Kate could write such a raunchy, hilarious novel? "It goes to show, Clyde, you can't judge a book by its cover." As Clyde snores gently, I turn Kate's book over in my hands and decide you probably *can* judge this book by its cover.

I stare out the window, feeling restless. Frustrated. Isolated. In a bigger city there'd be a vibrant nightlife, a pulsing heart of the city I could get lost in tonight, go wild in. But not in Mayton. Friday night at Café Diva was fun, but not exactly debauched. A shame. Right now, I feel like some debauchery wouldn't go astray.

I pull on my sneakers. "I need to run." Clyde gives a yawn and rolls onto his back. Within seconds he is asleep again, his white tummy exposed, pink paws in the air. I leave him behind and let myself quietly out of the house.

The night is clear and cold. My breath comes in puffs of white as I jog down the lane, turning left into Main Street. I will run through town to the river and back, that should be far enough to shake off this angst.

Halfway down Main Street, I'm surprised to hear someone call my name. I skid to a stop.

"Here! By the church."

I peer through the wrought-iron fence. "Billie?"

Billie makes a solemn bow and pitches herself into some lavender bushes. "Oops."

"What are you doing here?"

"Looking for..." Billie hiccups, scrabbling in the shrubbery. "Looking for my shoe."

"It's the middle of the night, how did you lose a shoe in the churchyard?"

She taps the side of her nose. "That's for me to know and you (hic) definnishly not to find out."

"I dunno, Bill, I can't find it on the path, I..." A short, blonde guy in a silver shirt appears out of the darkness. "Oh. Hi."

I recognise him as the guy I danced with at Café Diva before Johnny turned up. I take in the leaves in his hair and Billie's dishevelled appearance. "In a churchyard? Really?"

"Come on, Quinn, don't get preachy. Help me (hic) find my shoe."

"First time I've been called preachy. But in a churchyard, really." I scramble into the bushes with Billie and begin searching.

Silver Shirt looks sheepish. "We were having a few rounds at Mira's, then Bill said she'd walk me home. We heard an owl callin' in here. Bill wanted to see it so we sat down on the steps to watch for it and, well, one thing led to..."

"Mm." Billie grins. "It sure did. (hic) Shut up, Brad, Quinn doesn't want (hec) the details."

"Yep, I genuinely honestly don't."

"She's not interested in hearing about (hic) your (hec) conqueshts."

"Yep, I genuinely honestly am not."

Billie rummages. "She's only got eyes for (hic) one bloke anyway."

"Huh?" I sit up, rosemary twigs in my hair, and look at her.

"Found it!" Billie holds up a lone ballet flat in triumph.

"Good." Brad sounds impatient. "Now can we all go back to mine and get into the homebrew?"

"I'm not going to your place." I am staring up at the huge eucalypt tree standing by the church, its white trunk ghost-like in the garden lights.

Billie nods. "Yeah, Quinn was going (hec) for a run. But I'll come back to yours."

I shake my head slowly. "I'm going to climb that tree."

She follows my gaze. "Whoa. Seriously?"

I feel a sparkle of anticipation, my body coming alive like it hasn't in weeks. Well, not since Johnny's kiss, and I'm trying not to think too much of that. "Look at it, a perfect blue gum just waiting to be climbed."

"I dunno. In a churchyard and all."

I look at Brad. "Like you can preach."

Billie has put on her shoe and is beginning to catch my enthusiasm. "I don't think (hic) anyone's climbed this gum before. It'd be pretty cool."

"But it's so late! And that tree is huge! There's no way you two chicks can climb it."

Billie and I round on him. "You reckon?"

"Watch us."

He shakes his head. "No way. I'm not standin' round watching you two break your silly necks."

Billie glares, hands on hips. "Bradley Evans, you stay here and (hic) take a photo when I'm up there, otherwise Lollie (hec) won't believe it."

"Why not?" I circle the tree, looking for the best way up.

"Bill is scared of heights," he explains.

I stare at them. "How scared?"

They answer simultaneously, "Just (hic) a liddle bit."

"Lots."

"Hmm." I pause. "You don't have to come up, Billie."

Billie draws herself to full height. This is taller than Brad and I, but still doesn't amount to much. "Brad says I can't climb it, so I'm gonna."

"Alright, I admire a woman with balls, let's do it." I crouch, make a cup of my hands and boost her into the tree.

"Ooh."

I am encouraging. "It's not high. You're not even at the first fork yet. Start climbing."

"Yes, but ooh..."

"Close your eyes," I coax. "I'll guide you."

Brad's voice floats up. "I'm not standin' round down here watchin' you two..."

"Bradley Evans, don't you dare go home. Get your phone out (hic) I'm climbing!"

It takes a lot of encouragement and the occasional boost from me, but Billie soon gets as far up the tree as I judge it safe to go. Any further and the branches are getting too thin. I settle her into a comfortable fork and exhort her to open her eyes.

"Wow, I'm in the tree! Brad look, I'm in the tree! Yay no hiccups, this must've freaked 'em out and they left."

He sounds plaintive. "I *know* you're in the tree. And it's too dark for me to take a picture, you're way too small up there and way too high, the flash can't reach."

"Stop grumbling. Here, I'll stick my foot out, can you take a photo of that?"

I put out a warning arm. "Careful, Billie." I only met Billie on Friday night, I don't want her to fall out of a tree by Sunday morning.

"It's cool, Quinn, chill." She swivels. "Hey, I can see the church roof! Wow, totara shingles. I didn't know the church had a wooden Jesus carved into the gable, that must be 100 years old. An antique Jesus. My sisters would go nuts to see it..."

"I can't even see your foot, Bill," Brad complains. "There's no way I can take a photo of it."

"Forget it, I'll take a selfie." Billie has been clutching the tree with both hands, but now she begins rifling through her pockets for her phone.

"Watch you don't fall out." I'm beginning to realise it is not particularly relaxing climbing trees with other people, especially an intoxicated, purple-haired livewire like Billie Carlisle.

"I'll be fine. See? I'm not even scared of being this high. Must be because it's so dark. Ah, got it. If I lean out like this, I can get a selfie with all the leaves behind me..."

It was bound to happen. Had to, given Billie's inebriated state and the stories one hears of doomed selfie-takers the world over. Billie holds out the phone, drapes herself over a tree branch to get the perfect picture – and topples off.

Chapter 10

B illie screams. Already on my way to intervene, I launch myself as Billie falls and body slam her into the trunk. I wrap myself around Billie and the tree and hang on tight. "I've got you. Don't panic, I've got you!"

"Ohmigod ohmigod ohmigod ohmigod..." Billie is upside down and frantic.

"You shouldn't blaspheme like that in a churchyard, Bill, it's not..."

I yell, "Shut up down there, Billie's boyfriend, you are not helping!"

"Ohmigod ohmigod ohmigod..."

I try to soothe her. "OK, Billie, stop yelling. I need you to hold tight to me while I shift my leg like this, and my arm like *this* and give you room to..."

"I'm not moving, don't make me move!" Billie clutches me.

"But you're upside down, babe, that can't be comfortable. If I just move like..."

"Yeek," she yelps, "don't move!"

Brad interjects. "Bill, hurry up and get down here, it's cold and I wanna to go home."

She erupts, "Ohmigod Bradley Evans if I hear you grumbling one more time while I'm stuck up here in a tree nearly dying I will personally come down there and kick your..."

"Ask him to ring Johnny." I am panting with the effort of holding Billie's weight against the tree. I have one leg wedged in a fork, which hurts like hell, and the other wrapped around Billie. She is wriggling about so she can glare at Brad and not helping things one bit.

"What?" she asks.

My voice is hoarse with effort. "Ring Johnny. Get him to bring the ladder."

"But my phone fell down when I... Oh no! My phone fell! Brad, can you see my phone down there anywhere?"

I snap. "Get Johnny right *now* or I'll personally drop you so you can look for your phone yourself!"

Billie huffs. "You don't have to shout." She leans out again, endangering us both. "Brad, ring Johnny and get him to bring the big ladder."

"What? Why?"

"Because I am nearly dying here, that's why!"

"And me," I say.

"And Quinn." A pause. "No, really? But you're holding me up, you can't..."

Brad is still in the dark. "I gotta ring Johnny who?"

Billie explodes. "*Fireman* Johnny, you moron! Johnny Best, who has the bloody fire truck with the bloody ladder. Quinn has the hots for him and all the blokes in town have the hots for her so I'm sure he'll come straight away and..."

"Keep that up," I growl through gritted teeth, "and I'll push you out of this tree myself."

Billie wriggles round to stare up at me. I catch the scent of peach lip gloss as she grins suddenly. "This is crazy, huh? It's like we're in a movie."

"I... just need to know it's a comedy, not a tragedy."

She laughs. "I'd like to know that, too."

"Is your boyfriend calling the Fire Station?" I really, really need some hope right now.

"I think so. Brad is not my boyfriend but he's kinda cute, don't you think? Sometimes he seems pretty messed up, but then we all are, you know?"

I don't feel like answering. Hanging on for grim death, I know that if Billie lets go we'll both be more than pretty messed up.

"I like him," she muses. "He's hot. Maybe I'll ask him out. We've already consumay-what'samacallit in a churchyard (hic) so we might as well make it official. Damn, my (hic)cups are back."

"Billie is *where?*"

"Up a tree with that new chick, Flynn or Trin or..."

"Quinn." Johnny is patient. "Quinn Walker. She and Billie climbed a tree?"

"Well, yeah, I told them they couldn't climb it, it's too huge and Bill is scared of heights, but they did anyway and then Bill wanted a photo taken and she stuck her foot out but my flash couldn't reach far enough to take it and now Flynn or Trin or..."

"Quinn." There is an edge to Johnny's voice now. "What has happened, Brad? Tell me slowly. The whole thing." Sarah pokes her head round the door, curious, a little dishevelled by sleep. Johnny waves the phone and scowls.

"I don't know 'cos it's dark and they're really high but Bill freaked out and started blasphemin' like anything and then she said I have to call you to bring the ladder." He pauses to listen to some yelling in the background. "Quick. She says you have to bring the ladder quick."

"*Oddio*, is Quinn alright?" Johnny is moving now, heading for the truck bay.

"Well, she is yelling at Bill and Bill is yelling at me so I figure she's pretty good. You know, I don't see why Bill should be yelling at me when it's her who decided to do such a dumb…"

"Brad! Where are they?"

"In the tree."

Johnny is glad that Brad is on the other end of a phone call, not standing in front of him. There would be blood, definitely. And police involved. "Which tree, Brad? Where is it?"

"Oh, that big gum by the church on Main Street."

Johnny nods, as Sarah tosses him the keys. "I know it. We're on our way."

When the big truck rolls into the church carpark, I am never more glad of anything in my life. My muscles are burning, everything is aching and I'm terrified I'll drop Billie from sheer cramp and fatigue.

Johnny drives across the grass and parks up within ladder's reach of the tree. He switches on the spotlights on the side of the truck. I blink in the sudden glare and Billie swears.

As Sarah goes round to prep the ladder, Johnny strides to the base of the tree. "Are you alright?"

"Yes, but I'm freezing and I wanna go home."

"Not you, Brad. Quinn, are you alright?"

My voice is hoarse but I'm proud to find it is steady. "Yes. Billie fell. She's still kinda upside down and I've got her, but you need to be quick in case I drop her."

There is some frantic wriggling among the gum leaves. "Whaddya mean, you might drop me? Johnny, is that you? Hi, gorgeous. Get me the hell down, this is no picnic, I tell ya."

"Will do. Hang in there."

"Ha ha de ha."

As Johnny jogs back to the truck, I say, "Gorgeous?"

"Well, he is."

"Yes, but..."

"Don't panic, Quinn. I tried really hard but he never looked twice at me. Yay, here comes your knight in shining armour."

From my position clutching the tree it is difficult to see, but I hear Johnny directing Sarah at the ladder controls, asking her calmly to call the paramedics, and then speaking to Brad. Soon I feel his hand, steady and strong, on my leg.

"Quinn, how are you feeling?" Johnny's voice is gentle, professional.

"OK." I unaccountably want to cry. I am so emotional these days it's ridiculous. "Sore. Cold."

"You're doing an amazing job." He pauses to assess the situation. "Here's what is going to happen. First, I'll secure you both to the trunk with this harness. Then I'll take hold of Billie's shoulders to help you with the weight. That OK, Billie?

Between us, Quinn, we'll swing her round carefully so I can get her onto the ladder. Can you help me with that, do you think?"

"Yes." There must have been a wobble in my voice because Johnny's hand tightens briefly, reassuringly, on my calf. Then he unrolls a rope and reaches for Billie.

It is careful, painstaking, terrifying work, but between us we get Billie turned around, Sarah directing the lights from below. Johnny secures Billie to the ladder and guides her to ground level. As Sarah takes over, wrapping Billie in a blanket and handing her to the paramedics, Johnny climbs back up to me.

"Bella," he says gently.

I am huddled in the tree fork. "Dios mío, Johnny, I was so scared I would drop her!"

Johnny finds my hand, wraps it tightly in his. "Billie is safe. You did well to catch her. Now let's get you down safely."

I swallow my distress and follow his instructions. Johnny's voice is calm with a hint of gravel, his commands precise and professional as he fastens the harness and guides me gently down. I soon have my feet on firm ground.

I am shivering in my running shorts so Johnny slides a blanket round me. "The paramedics want to check you over."

"I'm fine, honestly. Just sore muscles."

"Multiple lacerations and contusions, possible hypothermia. You're going." Johnny steers me firmly towards the ambulance.

"OK, but Johnny?"

"Yes?"

"Gracias... I mean, grazie mille." A thousand times over, Johnny Best, thankyou.

"De nada," he says. The flash of a grin.

I laugh.

Johnny drives back to the Station with his head full of Quinn Walker. He sent Brad off, and Sarah said she'll stay and make sure Billie and Quinn get home OK. There is nothing more for Johnny to do, so he leaves.

Quinn. He cannot forget the sight of her white, frightened face in that tree. Brad had been inarticulate, so when Johnny reached the top of the ladder he was horrified to realise her predicament. With her arms and legs wrapped round Billie, hanging on for dear life, only Quinn's sheer strength and willpower was keeping them from falling. So small, yet indomitable. *Mamma mia.*

Johnny backs the truck into the bay, his hands deft on the wheel, his mind utterly somewhere else. Up in that tree, he had wanted to wrap himself around Quinn, take away her pain and fright, hold her and kiss her until everything was alright. Instead he had to tamp down his agonising fear, put on his professional voice and solve first one problem, then the next one and the next until he had them both safe on the ground.

He shuts down the engine and closes his eyes. It is terrifying to realise how much it would hurt now to lose Quinn. Ridiculous, because he hardly knows her. *It's been twelve years.* And also no time at all.

It will be hours before his heart stops racing and his body understands she is safe.

Later, when he's outside washing the engine, he spots Quinn climbing into her oak tree. She is carrying a book as usual, Clyde spinning around the trunk. She puts the book between her teeth so she can climb to the highest branch and he feels himself relax. Quinn is as irrepressible as ever. His world is alright.

Chapter 11

With barely four weeks until the Commemoration, Thea is keen to get some promotion underway. She calls a Council of War for Monday morning, at Gill's Hot Buns. About a dozen Mayton locals meet at the café tables.

I cause a minor stir when I turn up.

Sarah calls, "Did you like your view over the churchyard, Quinn?"

Lollie chimes in, "Billie is asking, will you take a selfie with her tonight in that big macrocarpa by the river?"

Grant laughs. "Good to see you, Quinn, thought you'd be at a branch meeting, ha ha, get it?"

"Very funny you lot." Thea glares at the hecklers and cuffs me lightly over the ear. "That's for dragging my boy and the truck out at 3AM." She grins. "And for the record, that was a helluva save."

"She wouldn't have been in the tree if not for me."

"Maybe, but it's Billie so you never know. Sit down here next to me. We have warm croissants and coffee, and Gill's muffins are to die for."

I dip my croissant in my coffee the way I learned in Italy, and listen to the hum of productive conversation. Billie turns up, nursing a hangover and minor lacerations. She kisses me on the cheek and sashays off to sit with Lollie. I relax and survey the tables.

Gill is there, round and dark to Sarah's leggy blonde, laughing and handing out food. Linc's elegant sister, Sue Brady is there, with a folio of promotional photos for Thea. Lollie waves her hands about as she describes the historical display she's set up in the library foyer, and the children's books about firefighters she's found for her reading sessions. Kate is there, checking the spelling on Thea's invitations. As she approves each one, Grant carefully rewrites it in his divine calligraphy.

Johnny is there. Yep, Johnny is there. Beyond that I can't say, my eyes are arrested by the sight of him. He is deep in conversation with Sarah and Linc about parade logistics, so I indulge myself a little and watch him. Today he is back in his uniform, with an official red and yellow badge on the arm. He looks tall and handsome, a little tired as usual. His mouth quirks up at something Linc says and he tips back on his chair, amused. His gaze ranges round the tables and settles on me.

His midnight eyes drag me in.

Glory, what a soul. His surges to meet mine like it has been waiting for this moment – and all the romantic woo woo Scarlett goes on about seems suddenly, stunningly real. Exciting, familiar, restless. I feel myself glowing with hope. Trust. Wanting. Right here in the bakery.

Johnny breaks eye contact. He mutters something to Linc and Sarah and they get up and go outside. Through the window I see them pacing Main Street together, deciding where the parade vehicles should start and finish, where the safety barriers should go.

I go back to my strawberry tea and macaroons. When it is time, I outline my plan for decorating the Station, and soon Thea's meeting agenda is complete. The little posse breaks up. Thea, Sue and Lollie head off with some staff members from the Council. The Carlisle sisters go back to their antique store. Kate tucks her arm in Linc's and bears him away.

Grant and Sarah climb into the fire truck. "Johnny, we're going round to Dave's Engineering to get the lockboxes fitted. Wanna come?"

"No," he says. "I'll walk back." The air brakes hiss as the truck moves away, and he turns his head slightly. "Quinn."

I am standing in the doorway, my heart pounding. "I need to thank you for last night."

"Just doing my job."

"Yes," I rasp, "but if you hadn't come to help us..."

"You'd have thought of something."

"You reckon?"

"I know." He studies me for a minute. "Come with me."

"Where?"

"The park. Something I want to show you."

I shut down my instinctive *No* to a man asking me to walk alone in the park with him. Johnny is in more danger from me than I'll ever be from him. "So long as we're not going to the rose garden."

"No roses." A smile flits through the words but doesn't reach his mouth.

We cross the street and enter the park. The garden beds bask and the oak avenue rustles gently in the mid-morning sunshine. Foliage glows with autumn colour. Now and then a leaf twirls to the grass, brushing our hair and our bodies on its downward eddy.

I catch one and study it, peppery black spots on gold. "Sad, when the leaves die."

"Sad when anything dies."

"True." I look at him, but Johnny is shuttered, walking fast. The park extends quite a distance, running parallel to Main Street behind the houses, almost as far as the Fire Station. I have to jog to keep up with him. I get the feeling Johnny is being drawn somewhere, perhaps reluctantly, and for some reason he's asked me along.

Just as I'm about to ask questions, Johnny ducks through a wooden gate into a little overgrown meadow. There, its branches spreading to the ground like a glorious green cavern, is a beautiful carob tree.

I realise now that this is not a meadow. It is the neglected backyard of Johnny's family home. "Ohmigod, I forgot about this tree!"

The quirk of a smile. "I thought you might like to see it again."

I part the branches to look inside. The tree cavern is cool and earthy. A couple of upturned crates and a filthy rug remain, decaying clues to our childhood adventures. "I loved this place so much, you can't imagine." I pause and think, perhaps you can. You still come here, Johnny Best. You were in the park that morning I got stuck in the roses.

Johnny is standing in the middle of the yard with his face turned to the sun. There is a stillness about him that makes my skin prickle. He has not brought me here just to see the tree. Why, then?

I hesitate. "Johnny, where is your brother? Does he still live in Mayton?"

"No. He died."

"Oh." In the accident Gill mentioned? I sit on the floor of the cavern and the tree sighs gently. I think of the whirlwind force of nature that was Mario Best, living life in the fast lane, beautiful and wild, impetuous. "How long ago?"

"Two years."

"You must really miss him."

Johnny is silent. I gaze about me through the fringe of leaves, remembering Johnny and his brother as teenagers – two tanned, active boys with dark hair flopping over their eyes and wide, flashing grins, Mario always ahead, laughing at Johnny, scrapping, competing, daring.

As my eyes adjust to the deep shade, I can make out the garage wall. I press my hand to its peeling timbers. Three planks are missing, just enough space for kids to wriggle through. And inside the garage... Oh, *inside*...

"*Ay*, it's that beautiful car!"

Johnny whips round. "Don't look in there."

"Why not? Look, here is Mario's car, all covered in dust!"

"Leave it. Come away."

"How could you let it get so..." I look at Johnny's face and realise I should have bitten my tongue. But now that I've seen Mario's car, I cannot look away.

Quinn looks so fierce she takes Johnny's breath away. She has seen the Pantera.

She cries, "It is so *beautiful*. How can you hide this away? It needs to be out in the sunlight, racing, growling, breathing."

His voice comes out harsh. "It is a car. It does not breathe."

Her eyes challenge him. "Do you really believe that?"

No, because my motorcycle breathes. It growls. It roars with joy when we race through the hills. "It is a car," Johnny says again. "It is safe here. Mario would not want it driven and damaged, or rusting in the rain."

"Mario wouldn't care for that. He used to drive it like the devil!" Quinn tilts her chin. "I don't agree with hiding it. Mario *loved* this car. He loved *you*! You were always scrapping, I know, but he was your *brother*. You should be letting this car live, not hiding it away!"

My brother. Gesu' Cristo.

We stare at each other, jagged memories of Mario between us.

The bleakness in Johnny's voice is even darker than his eyes. "What can you possibly know about it?"

I feel hot tears leaping to betray me. "Nothing. But I know *you*." I spin, and push between the planks. I slip past the sleek, red car and out through the door of the shed, glad that it's unlocked. I run across the lawn onto Main Street.

The daylight is blinding after the cool gloom of the tree. Johnny is in such a state that I cannot, *will* not let him see my weakness. My fear. My relentless desire. Perhaps even something like love.

I cross the road into Fire Station Lane, fleeing for the safety of the cottage. There, I can watch TV with Doris and make tea and pretend none of this has happened – that I never met up again with this beautiful, impossible, frustratingly annoying man.

I have a good headstart but he catches me at the gate. I have one hand on the latch, the other thrusting back the gate, when his strong hands enclose my waist. "Let me go!" He lifts me and I cut furious eyes to his. "How dare you, Johnny Best!" Then I see his face.

Johnny's gaze is seared with unshed tears – and something else, that thing I've seen before, so scorching and intense it strips my breath away.

He looks at me. I look back. His powerful hands are round my waist and my feet are off the ground but I am not afraid of him. His body feels warm and strong and all I can do is stare into those tortured, midnight-blue eyes.

"Don't run." His voice is like a rasp over fire-hardened oak. "Please."

I nod. "OK."

"I was wrong. You are right about Mario. The car. But this is..." he swallows. "Hard for me."

I bring my hands to his face, touch the rough slant of his jaw. "You can put me down now."

"Oh. I'm sorry." He sets me on my feet, his cheeks flushing crimson. I catch a fleeting glance of that awkward, embarrassed teen I knew so many years ago.

I can feel every part of my body where it met his. "Now please, Johnny, please. Kiss me."

"What, now?" Johnny can't breathe. He doesn't know if he will be able to stop at just one kiss. He considers flight – instant, life-preserving flight. International. Intergalactic, perhaps. Yes, safer.

"Now. Please."

Quinn is still touching his face. He surrenders and kisses her.

If I thought our first kiss was spectacular, it is nothing compared to this one. As Johnny leans in there's a communion between us that sends lightning to every nerve end. His eyes widen with mine. *Ohhh.*

I stand on tiptoes and he deepens the kiss. Cupping my face with his hands, his thumbs caress my cheekbones and his mouth commandeers mine. He is strong, demanding and gentle, all at once. I close my eyes, feeling his lashes soft on my skin, his touch even softer, a butterfly trace taunting me. *Ay.* Johnny's mouth was made for kissing. He has a major talent here that has been inadequately explored.

I want more of this. I want *more.* But Johnny is breathing hard and perhaps not for the same reason I am, because I can feel him drawing away. "Johnny, stay!"

He shakes his head and stumbles off down the lane. He does not look back.

After a moment of indecision, I decide not to follow. Instead, I pirouette up the porch steps and hug myself in the hall. What a kiss. And what a man! Oh yes, I definitely want more of that.

Chapter 12

It is not clear to me how I get through the rest of my week. At the end of it, I can't remember a single piece of work I've completed. Whose plans have I signed off on? Whose ideas have I turned into concept drawings this week? Watermill House is almost at completion, but it could have evolved from a Victorian era restoration into brutalist architecture for all I can recall.

What is clear is that Johnny is not rushing back into my arms. I catch his eye on my way down the lane, early on Wednesday morning, and he gives me the tiniest smile but he does not put down his spanner and he does not leave his fire engine to come fire me up instead.

On Friday morning, he touches my hand by accident when he returns my escapee collie. I feel the brush of his skin and rejoice in the hot tingle that shoots to my navel. Does he hesitate? Maybe. But he slips his hand from mine and goes immediately back to the Fire Station.

I jog home with Clyde, thinking I *must* find a way in. If he can kiss me like that, there is something, I know it. Unless of course, he kisses everyone like that.

That is something to consider. I decide on reflection it's unlikely. If Johnny kisses everyone like that, the entire cohort of emotionally-available women in Mayton would've gone supernova by now and the town would be a blasted wreck.

Johnny is not at Café Diva on Friday, but the general populace is partying on much like they did last week, with no colossal explosions or interstellar shockwaves. The only shockwave is within my own heart. I realise I am beginning to enjoy living here. I don't want to leave.

Johnny is horrified at what he did to Quinn. He chased her, grabbed her, overpowered her and kissed her. He is so ashamed. Of course, she *told* him to kiss her. And she begged him to stay when he broke the kiss. But that is not the point. He behaved impulsively and was so angry, so demanding, that of course she'd want to pacify him. Had he frightened her? How terrible if he had.

He studies his hands in the dim glow of the Station's security lights. He is so big and hulking, and she is so small and light. How could he not have frightened her?

Johnny straightens his shoulders, sets his jaw. He's been a week agonising about it but there is nothing else to do. He must apologise to Quinn. He swings his feet off the cot and heads for the door before his nerve fails him. It is not too late. Her light is on so she'll be up. Her night routine is as familiar to him as his own.

When Johnny's boots hit my front porch, I am lying in bed staring at the ceiling and trying not to think of him. I've almost convinced myself that I don't need him, when he thumps on the door.

Clyde leaps up, barking. My heart leaps, too. No one else thumps on my door quite like that. I run into the hall and flick on the porch light. *Yes!* No one else fills my doorway quite like that, either.

I take a moment to tidy my ponytail and smooth my shirt. I listen for Doris, but she hasn't woken. She never does before midnight. I am barefoot, in grey leggings and an oversized, pink pyjama shirt with a teddy bear on the front, but that can't be helped. Johnny is at my door! I know without doubt that if I am slow to answer, he will bolt and never come back.

I fling open the door. "Hello!" My beam of welcome flickers a little when I see his expression. Johnny looks like he is here for a funeral, not coming in panting haste to kiss me again.

"Hello, Quinn." Clyde darts out and does a delighted lap around him, but Johnny barely gives him a glance.

"You look like you need to come in." I open the door wider. "In fact, you look like you need a drink." Come in, have anything. Have it all.

"I won't stay."

I shake my head. "Stay, Johnny Best, or I'll be offended."

"You will?"

"Yes, you always leave! I'd like you to come in this time."

"Alright."

But he looks so miserable, my heart sinks. "OK, tell me the bad news."

"Pardon?"

"Give me the bad news. I was hoping this was a social visit, but you obviously have something terrible to impart so let's get it over with. Is it the Morris? Do you want my firewood back?"

Johnny stares at me. "There is no bad news, Quinn. I just want to apologise to you."

"Apologise? What for?"

"I am very sorry for the way I treated you the other day."

"When?"

"On Monday, when I chased you and..."

"What are you talking about? Why would you apologise for that?"

"Well, I manhandled you and... took liberties. I *kissed* you."

"You're apologising for kissing me?"

"Well, yes, I feel bad about it."

I want to laugh but I mustn't. "I'm sorry you feel bad about kissing me, Johnny, because I have not been able to think about anything else all week. I want you to kiss me again. I really, *really* want you to kiss me."

Johnny is staring at his feet, but he moves his gaze now to my feet. His eyes travel slowly up my body. "Really?"

I feel sparkly, reckless, delighted. "I wouldn't say it if I didn't mean it."

"You are not mad at me? You weren't... afraid?"

"Are you kidding? Just kiss me already."

Johnny swallows and I close the gap between us. I stand on tiptoes and run my hands over his shoulders. The warm bulk of him, that ripple of muscle as he moves his hands to the small of my back sends a squirm of desire through me. He kisses me, his mouth gentle, his stubbled chin rough against mine.

"More," I whisper, and I feel his mouth curve up in a grin. As his tongue slides between my teeth I feel him tasting, exploring, demanding. Desire rushes in.

I am oblivious to time. I am oblivious to the small pool of light we are standing in, on my grandfather's creaking porch. Clyde is at our feet and my step-grandmother is sleeping at the other end of the hall, but Johnny fills my space and my senses, his arms round me and his mouth on mine and flaming heat between us.

After a minute, hours, perhaps days I do not know, Johnny releases me. He kisses me on the nose and steps back. Breathing hard, he rubs his hand through his hair. "Well, Quinn Walker."

"Well." I gaze at him. My heart is racing. Would it be precipitous if I undressed him right here on the porch?

"Notte."

Goodnight? I dart forward but he is gone, taking the steps in one stride, clicking the gate shut behind him in the night. What the...?

I didn't get him in for a drink, or for anything at all. And he didn't even notice my teddy bear pyjamas, let alone try to take them off me. I am not sure whether to be relieved or insulted.

Later, tossing in bed while Clyde snores, I decide it might have been for the best. I figure if Johnny runs like that after kissing me, he might've died of shock if I'd invited him in to have my way with him. A pity. Desire twists in the pit of my stomach as I recall the touch of his mouth, his strong hands at my waist.

Surely there will be another chance? There must be. I can see I may have to ramp things up a notch. I want this man with his crooked grin and his scar, his warm strength and monosyllabic reserve. I have never been so sure of anything.

Chapter 13

Doris's friend Shirley comes as manna from heaven. I didn't know she existed, and when she turns up at the door this week it seems like Doris doesn't know she exists, either. After a brief, confused conversation she recalls Shirley to mind and greets her with delight. Apparently, this lovely friend has been away for several months visiting her daughter in England. Now she is home, Shirley has heard about Alfred and wants to help keep an eye on Doris.

I study Shirley with interest. She looks about Alfred's age, mid-seventies. She is a retired school principal, outgoing where Doris is reserved and decisive where Doris overthinks. Both have intelligent, enquiring minds so I can see why they get along.

Shirley has decided what Doris needs is a weekend in Wellington to clear the cobwebs. I'm not sure quite what that entails, but because what I need is a weekend free of Doris, I am very encouraging. I brew Earl Grey tea while they discuss whether to catch a movie at the Lighthouse cinema, the Embassy or the Roxy, Shirley's membership tickets for the ballet, and the best hotel to stay in.

It is decided that I will drop them at the train station midday Friday, and pick them up sometime on Sunday. They'll ring to let me know which train they'll be on.

Perfect. I know exactly what I want to be doing for the hours in-between.

Johnny is stretched out under the fire engine when Quinn walks in off Main Street, a diminutive figure framed by the huge roller door. He catches her silhouette in the corner of his eye and drops his wrench.

"Good morning." Her voice is light.

He rolls onto one elbow and rasps a reply. He doesn't know what, he just hopes it was in English.

"Are you on duty Friday night?"

Hope leaps in Johnny's chest. He clamps his jaw tight to stop it showing in his face. "No."

"Come for dinner, then." She tips her head sideways, birdlike. "Doris is going away for the weekend, and I owe you a drink. Around seven?" Johnny nods and rolls back under the truck.

"Right." Quinn whistles for Clyde and walks home.

It takes some effort to find the ingredients for paella marinera in Mayton, but I manage it. I track down saffron, chorizo and piquillo peppers from a specialist deli Thea recommends, and fresh seafood from the truck that visits twice a week. I choose a sauvignon blanc to match, and go to Gill's Hot Buns for fresh bread.

The biggest problem is deciding what to wear. My fashion statement needs to be sexy enough to give Johnny the idea, but not so revealing that it scares him off. He is, I have found, inclined to bolt for cover.

Midmorning on Friday I climb into my tree and reread the first eight chapters of Lady Hatwick's lace-frilled adventures. I come down to earth inspired. In my wardrobe I have a flouncy, thigh-length dress with lace sleeves and a tiered hem. It is firehouse red, with demure little white flowers dotted over the bodice. It shows enough leg to be interesting and I won't wear shoes, I'm going for a casual Mediterranean style.

I take Doris and her friend to the station and wave them off. I do my meal preparation in jeans and a sweatshirt, and at a quarter to seven I change into my dress. Standing on the edge of the bath to check my reflection, I decide to leave my hair down and add sparkly stud earrings.

It is lucky I have a good fire burning in the kitchen. I hadn't realised how cold my dress and bare feet would be in autumn, in Mayton. I sprint from the frigid bathroom to the warm kitchen, hear Johnny's thunderous knock on the front door and run out again to answer it.

Johnny looks gorgeous. Heart-stoppingly, show stoppingly, downright gorgeous. He is wearing dark Levis and a green marle crewneck sweater under his leather jacket. Of the three buttons on his waffle knit, two are open, showing olive skin at his throat. I stand in my doorway and drink him in.

"Quinn." Johnny holds out a box of chocolates. I stand still, staring, until Clyde barks.

I pull myself together and open the door wide. "Good evening, Johnny, come in." His jacket brushes me in the doorway and I breathe him in. I've never noticed how divine he smells. Leather, citrus and indefinable sexiness.

My kitchen seems smaller with Johnny in it. This is not a negative. Clyde dances around us as I reach for the wine. "Would you like a drink?"

He nods, hanging his jacket on the hook and taking a seat by the fire with Clyde. I hand him his glass, and as I turn away his fingers brush my dress. "This looks nice."

"Thankyou." I resist the urge to climb into his lap and invite his closer inspection. "I bought this dress in Granada when I lived there for a few months. Didn't love the weather though."

His eyes crinkle. "Hot in summer, freezing in winter."

"You've been there?"

"Mamma sent Mario and I to Catanzaro to meet all her family."

I wait a beat, then decide he needs prompting questions. "How did that go?"

"Zia Stella kept trying to marry us off, so we went to Gambarie to ski. Then we bought a van and went travelling, didn't come back for three years." He gets up to take the cutlery and sets the table while I check on the paella.

"So, you're a Calabrian?"

"My mother's family. My father was English, I don't think you met him."

"That explains your English surname. How did they meet?"

"In Italy, while he was on a diplomatic posting. Mamma followed him to Wellington."

"It was a big move for her, so far from home and family."

"She was in love." Johnny shrugs like it's a simple thing. "Zia Rosa came over a few years later. The family were not happy about it."

"I can imagine! Family is everything to a Calabrian."

"And stubbornness." There's his smile. "Zia Stella still rings Rosa every few weeks to demand her sisters come home." And a shadow. I wonder if there is something he's not saying.

My paella is almost done. I toss it with a spatula and bring the hot pan to the table. "This is a Spanish meal and I'm sharing it with an Italian, but what the hell, we're in New Zealand. Buon appetito."

"Grazie, anche a te." We eat directly from the shallow pan, cracking open the scallop shells, letting their warm juice run down our wrists, and tearing the fresh bread with our hands. Once, he catches me watching him and his smile crooks.

I say, "This would taste better cooked over an open fire."

"It is perfect. But I could light the fire tower for you."

"I could cook a mighty paella on that!"

"No, next time I must cook for you." I catch the quicksilver blink of Johnny's eyes, as though he has surprised even himself with his offer. This guy has more layers than an onion. A million questions leap to mind but I stamp them down, reaching instead for the wine bottle. Am I learning reticence? Soon I'll be completely civilised.

Johnny has explained 'this' is difficult for him. It is obvious that not all his scars are visible ones, and I do not want to drive him away. I feel graceful and sparkling in my red dress, I am proud of my hospitality, and not even Clyde's unsubtle demand for extra dinner can dent my mood tonight.

When I get up to remove the paella pan, Johnny stands, too. He is close, and I reach for his hand. His fingers wrap round mine like a man drowning. I can barely breathe, I want him so much. He lifts my hand and kisses it, a fleeting caress.

A phone jangles in the depths of Johnny's jacket, by the door.

He looks at me helplessly. "I must answer it. The ring tone, I know it's..." He finds the phone. "Ciao, Zia Rosa." In a moment Johnny frowns, rattles off a stream of Italian I have no hope of following, then turns to me. "Mamma's had a turn and my aunt has called the ambulance. I will meet them at the hospital." He looks at the remains of our meal, the half-full bottle of wine. "I am sorry. I don't know how long I'll be."

Johnny flinches at the disappointment in Quinn's face but she says, "No hay problema. Oh god, sorry," and jogs down the hall to switch on the porch light. "Is there anything I can do?"

He wants to say, *Come with me. Mamma hasn't spoken to me in two years and she may not even know you're there, but I will. I need you. You make everything better.* But that would sound ridiculous, so he shakes his head and walks into the rain.

It is the work of a few minutes to grab his gear from the Station and roll his bike out. The headlamp lights up the raindrops, casting wild shadows as he rumbles onto Main Street. He feels the tug of that firelit kitchen and that beautiful, sparkling woman – *Mamma mia*, Quinn can cook – then a ripple of anxiety. Rosa had sounded very distressed. He opens the throttle on the highway south into the hills.

I listen for his motorcycle all through watching a movie with Clyde, then playing with him in the garden. I consider ringing Az to while away the time, but she's been quiet lately and I don't know where to start. So much has happened, so much has changed. The lights of the Station dance on my wall as I undress. I slip my teddy bear shirt over my breasts and pull flimsy shorts over my knickers. They are red lace knickers, chosen to match the dress I wore so beautifully, but this is useless information to anyone but myself, it seems. Frustration and unrequited passion surge.

"This is abominable," I tell Clyde as I climb into bed. "I was all dressed up and sure I had him. Now he's gone and I don't even know if he likes me." Wants me. "Maybe he is just being polite?"

I think again of Johnny's hands, that hooded gaze and his beautiful mouth. If he continues to insist on being polite I will be seriously disappointed.

Johnny is gone all night and the next day. It is dark again and has been for hours when he rumbles quietly into the lane, trying not to disturb the sleeping townsfolk. His bike is not the sort that is ever really quiet, though. As the Harley rolls into the stationyard, I hear the throb of its V-twin through my feet. I tell Clyde to stay, and run barefoot in my pyjamas into the night.

The cobblestones feel slick and cold. I follow the tail-light of Johnny's bike, standing in the drizzle while he settles the Harley on its kickstand and removes his helmet.

He turns to see me at the shed door. "Quinn. It's late and it's raining. You're soaked."

"I heard your bike. How's your mamma?"

He is gruff. "She is fine. Stable. But she had another small attack so they're keeping her in again tonight."

"That must be a worry for you."

A worry? Johnny stares at Quinn. He can't believe she is out here, standing in the rain. He should say something. "It is her heart." *It is broken.* "I am sorry our dinner was interrupted, you went to a lot of trouble."

"I don't care." She follows him to the back step of the Station as he drags off his heavy wet-weather jacket. "Family is more important."

Johnny nods. "Quinn, please go home, you must be cold." *Please. You look so beautiful standing in the rain, with that teddy bear clinging to every curve. If you stand this close for much longer I'll be having to apologise to you again.*

"Come with me," she says.

"Pardon?" Midway through changing his boots, Johnny's eyes cut to mine.

I want to throw myself into his arms, kiss some of the pain from his exhausted face and try to wrest back the magic. "Come home with me. Please." Because you look so sad and I want you. Really want you. "You came to dinner. Come back and finish it. Have dessert. Coffee. Anything."

Please yes, anything. Even if I'm no longer in my red dress, anything would be good.

Johnny puts his wet boots inside the porch. He hangs his jacket on a hook and hesitates, like he's trying to decide something. I hug myself. It *is* cold, even standing here under the eaves. "Johnny?"

The longing in his eyes is so startling and blatant that I catch my breath. He *does* want me. What is he waiting for? "OK, I'm going home now and I want you to come. Don't think about it, just do it." I grab his hand and step off the porch.

We're halfway across the stationyard when the rain starts to pelt down. I break into a run. Dragging Johnny behind me, I sprint for my house. In a moment he overtakes me and lifts me on the run, swooping me through the gate and onto my deck.

Laughing, I open the door and Clyde dives out. "Look Johnny, your crazy canine friend wants to say hello, *down* Clyde, honestly he's unstoppable, it's like he has a supercharger under the hood." I give the dog a moment, then slide into Johnny's personal space. "Let me explain something to you..." I really, really like you. I want to seduce you, totally and unashamedly, right now.

I look into his eyes and don't know where to start. After a moment's hesitation, Johnny wraps me in his arms. His linen shirt and my soaked cotton teddy bear steam gently.

"I don't have the words for this." I grab a fistful of Johnny's shirt and drag him inside.

Chapter 14

In the hall, I ask, "May I?" He nods wordlessly, and I run my fingers up his arms to his biceps. Goosebumps trail across his skin at my touch. *You want me, I know it.* His damp shirt clings to his muscled chest. He is so masculine and beautiful. On tiptoes, I reach to cup his jaw. Does he flinch? OK, no touching his face then.

"Kiss me," I say huskily. His answering kiss is as flammable as ever. I decide there is no time like the present, even in teddy bear pyjamas. I press my palms to his chest and walk him backwards into my room.

Johnny wraps his arms around me and I come smack up against his bulk. It feels like hitting a brick wall. "I don't know if this is a good idea," he rasps.

"Why not?"

"I could hurt you. You barely know me, I..." He just stands there, holding me. I can't see his face.

I am trying to think, and fast. If Johnny keeps worrying like this I'll never get his kit off him. "OK. I don't believe you'll hurt me, but I'll tell you straight away if you do. And you can promise to stop if it seems like I'm not having a good time."

"Yes. Of course."

"Good." I wriggle out of his grip and put his hands to my breasts. "Now you touch me *here* and I'll touch you *there*, and we'll see where it takes us." Because I want you. All of you. Now.

I grip his crotch, feel him suck air and harden up. With my other hand I lift my shirt. His hands slide under the pink teddy bear, his thumbs brushing the curve of my breasts. My skin lights up and his eyes meet mine, flaring with lust. I back him urgently to the bed. He has his mouth on me, I'm tugging at his belt. I push him onto the bed and haul off his jeans. He is powerfully muscled, his abdominals rippling as he helps me remove his shirt. I pause to drink in the sight of him.

He reaches up, smiling, and pulls me down beside him. His skin is cold from the rain but he feels delicious. I slip my hand inside his boxers and he makes a guttural sound of pleasure. Somewhere at floor level, Clyde whines.

"Ohmigosh, I forgot the dog." I grab Clyde and hustle him out to his mat by the kitchen fire. I give him a pat and a biscuit. "Stay, I'll be back soon." Hopefully not too soon. I shut the door firmly.

Johnny is sitting naked on the bed, untying his boots in the lamplight. I am caught between laughter at this absurdity, and delight that this gorgeous man is here doing anything at all. "Let me help." I pull off the left one, then the right. I slide between his knees. My breasts are on his thighs, his body hair rough on my tongue as I kiss my way over his torso.

He runs his hands over my teddy bear, lingering on the best parts. His touch is electric and I am on fire. He tugs at my shirt. Take it off? Yes definitely, please please. The teddy bear slips to the floor and his broad, blunt hands are on my body, rubbing and teasing. He kisses my mouth, my throat, my breasts. I moan, and feel a warm puff of breath in response. I think it's a laugh. Pleasure. Wanting.

I shake out my ponytail and his eyes glow with lust. He thrusts his fingers deep in my hair, gripping the nape of my neck. I skim my tongue over his body, tracing a line of fire from his breastbone to his hips. He moans and pulls me close. I am teasing now, pulling, tasting. He trembles, his breath coming hard.

"Quinn, please." He scoops me onto the bed beside him, slides one hand under my bum and his tongue under my lacy knickers. I relax and let him play. Gentle at first, then commanding, he eases my desire into a rippling wave of pleasure. I am sure my cries can be heard all the way down Fire Station Lane but I really don't care. I bury my fingers in his hair and let him please me.

I am soon breathless and gasping, and it takes me a moment to remember Johnny. I reach into a bedside drawer and pull out a packet. He kisses me, eases on the condom and I push him against the headboard. He is hard, quivering muscle in my hands.

I crawl into his lap and his eyes darken. Lust. Need. Wanting. His hands wrap my waist and I shift a little, experimentally. He moans and tightens his grip. Our mouths and bodies meet. I wrap my legs around him, his cheek stubble rough against my skin, our breathing mingled. Desire surges hot and fierce. We move together, his mouth on my breasts, my hair in his eyes, until we are whitehot with sex and sweat and suspended reality.

I hold him tight, breathing hard, until the world intrudes again. A branch rubs on the porch roof. The Station lights dapple my wall.

He eases out gently, kisses me. Midnight eyes meet mine. "Quinn." The way he says it, my name is a caress.

"Mm, Johnny." My face feels flushed, my whole body is tingling. "You can come anytime. Seriously. Do that again and I'll have to take you to meet my mother."

Johnny laughs, and I delight in it. He has a rich, generous laugh and I want to hear it again. Heaven help me I am in so much trouble.

I trace lazy whorls on his chest. "Now, how about that drink?"

It feels odd inviting Johnny, in his jeans again, to sit at Doris's table after we've just had sex in my grandfather's library. But this is a fractional discomfort outweighed by sheer, giddy pleasure. "White wine? There's some left in the bottle. Red wine, beer, caffeine?"

Johnny places his hands on the table and looks at me. His dark hair is tousled, his brows sweeping over long, thick lashes. His expression is pensive. Could it be regret?

To take it away I say impulsively, "You have beautiful eyes. And a beautiful smile, you should smile more." I think of Billie and Lollie. "Or maybe not. Women will swoop in from all over town and you'll have nothing left for me."

His smile flashes. "Coffee."

"Good choice. If we start on the alcohol, who knows what it might lead to." I hum as I put the kettle on, find coffee mugs and let Clyde into the garden.

Johnny's eyes roam over the kitchen, the woodburner, rag rug and wood box, linger on the kitchen cupboards.

I say, "Alfred had those painted recently, know anything about that?"

Midnight eyes fix mine. "Yes."

"Did you paint the garage, too?" He ducks his head in acknowledgement and I feel a rush of gratitude. Doris had bristled, but Alfred liked the young guy. I could imagine Johnny turning up, listening silently to his instructions, then getting to work. I grin. "Doris said you kept on painting until the paint ran out." Of course. It's the kind of thing Johnny would do.

"The garage was looking rough, it needed a clean-up. But the kitchen was just for fun."

How could Johnny articulate the homeliness, the peace he had felt, painting this little kitchen while summer light danced in the windows? He'd enjoyed working here, with the young dog trotting busily in and out, Alfred bringing him iced drinks and chattering about his beloved granddaughter, that little gadabout who was travelling the world, sending postcards from places Alfred couldn't pronounce. It was the first news Johnny had heard of Quinn in twelve years.

Instead, he fondles the dog's ears and lets Quinn talk. It is warm in the kitchen and Johnny's blood is still running hot, he doesn't really need the fire. At first this evening, he was startled by Quinn's forthrightness, but now he realises she's always been like that. It is one of the best things about her. Quinn knows what she wants and is not afraid to ask for it. Tonight, he was more than happy to oblige.

Oblige. What a word. It is totally inadequate to describe how he feels. He'd charge into a burning building for her.

He flinches. It is perhaps not a good example.

I set down the coffee mugs and see him flinch, catch the tightening of his jaw. "Milk?" He shakes his head, so I pour some into mine and add sugar. After all this exercise, I deserve it. I slide my hand into Johnny's, absorbing the warmth and strength of him. The planes of his face soften slightly.

I suck down coffee to distract myself from climbing into his lap and going for it, right here in front of Clyde. I need to be a responsible dog parent, but this is all very difficult. I'm not sure either how Johnny will respond. I jumped on him the minute he got in the door. Would twice in one night be welcome, or overdoing it?

I try to read him. Johnny is drinking his coffee and watching the dog, his hand still in mine. I let the quiet of the room wash around us until I can't stand my curiosity any longer.

"Johnny," I say. He looks at me. "I'm trying to work something out here. You seem very nice," *gentle*, I want to say. "You used to help Alfred, you still look out for his dog every day, you rescued Billie and I from that tree with no judgement..." He quirks a brow and I grin, "Well, none that you expressed to me, so... Why did you think tonight that you might hurt me?"

Johnny turns my hand over, traces my palm with his thumb. His touch sends butterflies through me but I try to stay focussed. "I am big, and you are so small."

"That's all?"

A smile. "You are stronger than you look, bella."

"You'd better believe it." But I'm not convinced that is the reason. "I warn you though, I don't like spiders. And those rose thorns I fell into were next level."

He laughs, and I can't help myself. I jump up and come round the table and enfold him in a hug from behind. "I am glad you're here."

He spins in his chair, catches my mouth with his and kisses me, hard. "So am I." His voice is husky. I lean in, and he slides his hands to my hips. He raises an eyebrow and I nod, so his hands ride under my shirt. I am gloriously naked under there, and his touch is electrifying.

"Clyde," I bark, and run the dog into the hall. I shut the door while the collie looks up at me. *Make up your mind!* Stifling a giggle, I crush any parenting guilt and pirouette back to the table. "Where were we?"

Johnny pushes back his chair and I ease onto his lap. I wriggle against the bulge in his jeans, settle in a little deeper. "Mmm..." He cups my buttocks, buries his face in my hair and lets me rock myself to pleasurable gasping. Then he slips his hands up again, teasing my nipples fleetingly, kissing my face. My voice is hoarse, "Your turn?"

He shakes his head. *That's the rattle of the Station door. The engine is going out, so the siren will sound soon.* "This is enough for me. More than enough."

He holds me. I can feel his heartbeat against my ribs, and hear it, deeper and slower than mine. I let my breathing slow to match his.

The loud, drawn-out howl of the Station siren splits the night silence. It roars mightily throughout the villa, shattering the quiet. In the hall, Clyde lifts his nose and howls along with it.

Johnny tucks a stray lock of hair behind my ear. "I have to go, bella."

"OK." I shrug my shirt straight. I can taste his mouth on mine, feel his hands on my body and his passion on my soul. He rinses his coffee mug and leaves, closing the door gently behind him. I run two joyous laps of the back lawn, with Clyde barking beside me, and fall into bed.

I sleep like the dead until the dog wakes me at first light, and Doris phones to tell me which train she'll be on.

Chapter 15

Johnny smiles to hear the excited barking of the dog mingled with the howl of the siren. Quinn's scent is on his skin, her urgent need seared like a brand on his mind. He sets off down the lane to work. Tonight did not go anything like he expected. He'd genuinely thought he was there for coffee, a kiss if he was lucky. He is not sure what to think about it all, but he isn't complaining.

Riding in the fire truck to the accident, he gets to thinking. What does Quinn want from him, going forward? What she wanted tonight was obvious. He hopes, with a frisson of anxiety, that he satisfied her. He has no idea about the future.

What does he want? He wants Quinn. He always has. His attraction to her was instant and primal, so many years ago, and is still whitehot and impossible. He can't have a woman in his life. How will he keep her safe?

He rubs his hand through his hair. This is confusing. Terrifying. *Quinn Walker*. The woman is so deep under his skin, it's going to hurt like hell to get her out.

At the accident scene, the police direct them straight to the rolled vehicle. Johnny takes over from Grant to manoeuvre the truck as close as possible. The waterlogged ground is treacherous where the single vehicle rollover has cut up the track and the riverbank, so he's careful where he parks.

Sarah, Grant and Jem leap out. They work fast to get the Jaws of Life set up and begin cutting into the stricken vehicle. Johnny stays with the truck, illuminating the scene with spotlights and bringing them tools as they need. They are working hard to free the trapped driver.

The job is about half done, Grant just beginning to peel back the roof, when Johnny feels a shifting under his feet. Startled, he looks up to see a huge slice of the riverbank beginning to calve off into the fast-moving current. Sarah, Grant, Jem and the rolled vehicle are on that bank. It is dark, the movement obscured by shadows and the flashing lights of emergency vehicles, but he can see the danger.

The river is running high after recent autumn rains. Johnny feels dread in the pit of his stomach. He shouts a warning to his team, sees Sarah catch his alarm. The bank is collapsing faster now. The vehicle, the trapped driver and three firefighters begin to tumble as the riverbank folds in on itself.

Johnny grabs a coiled rope from the truck. With all his strength, he casts it to Sarah just as the bank slides out from under them. He feels their sudden weight as they grab the rope and he reefs it round a cleat on the truck. The rope bounces tight, as taut as the fear thrumming through Johnny. He leaps into the driver's seat and slams the truck into reverse. The truck wheels churn up the soft mud of the bank, and slowly Johnny hauls them to safety.

When his team are free of the current, he parks up. He runs to help them out of the water. Water tugs with persistent fingers as he grasps cold hands, wrists, anything, and pulls hard.

When they are out, Sarah clutches at him. "Thanks, Johnny, that was close, it happened so fast!"

The three firefighters turn to watch the doomed car. Just its roof is now visible as it spins slowly in the water and slides under the surface. Bystanders are shouting in alarm, and several police officers begin urgently discussing a rescue but Johnny knows it is impossible. The man was trapped. They were unable to free him in time and it is certainly not possible now, beneath that torrent of dirty water.

He feels sick. There are tears in Grant's eyes, and Sarah and Jem look stricken. Johnny scrubs at his face tiredly and goes looking for any gear that's been spared by the river.

The truck lights cast weird shadows over the water and bounce bright colours off the trees. It is a surreal and silent scene despite all the activity. The river has claimed a helpless soul and it swirls endlessly onwards in implacable disregard for the shock and sorrow left behind.

Johnny works in a daze. His team does a quick debrief with police at the scene, and promise to give formal statements in the morning. Johnny drives in silence back to the Station and they begin unpacking the gear. No one seems to want to talk. When they've finished their tasks, his colleagues peel quietly off to go home.

"Bye, mate. Thanks."

"Yeah, thanks. Bloody hell."

"Love you, Johnny." That's Sarah, who's seen the darkness in his eyes.

"Yeah." Johnny stands alone on the back step of the Station and watches the night sky wheel above him.

Quinn's cottage is quiet, the windows dark. He wants to climb into her bed, pull her into his arms and hold her tight until this sick, sad feeling goes away. He knows he will feel better with her body against his, their fingers entwined, the sweet scent of her in every breath. He cannot believe that just a few hours ago he was in her bed, absorbing every atom of her passionate energy and forthright heart.

He takes a deep, shuddering breath. *Loss. Pain.* The events of tonight have brought him right back to the horror of the night he lost Mario. This time, he acted fast enough to save the team from disaster. But he could not save everyone. Just like that night when he was unable to save his brother.

Into this night comes the roar of an engine. With a skitter of tyres, Thea's station wagon bumps up the kerb. She runs into the yard, pulls up short when she sees him. Her eyes are wide, her hair dishevelled. "My god, Johnny, what a night you've had! Sarah told me what happened."

"Thea." He lets her hug him.

"I've been round to see the others, they are feeling OK, given the circumstances. I'll ask a counsellor to come in the morning." Thea blows out her cheeks, scrubs a hand through her curls. "Jeeze that was close. It could've been really bad. They had all their gear on, and the river is so deep there..."

"It *was* bad. We lost the driver of the car."

"I know." She bows her head. "I know. But we could have lost all of them." She reaches out, her hand warm on his. "Are you alright? You were amazing. You saved three lives tonight."

Johnny's gaze is steady, but inside is a deep, deep sadness. It breaks Thea's heart to see it because she knows she cannot help him. She cannot take away that pain and loss, she cannot bring Mario back. "Is your mamma OK?" she asks at last.

"She is stable. The doctors say she can go home tomorrow." *Home? Actually, to Rosa's home.*

Thea hesitates. "Should I stay? Will you be alright tonight?"

"I'm alright."

She gazes at him for a moment, then leans in and kisses his cheek. "Goodnight, Johnny."

"Goodnight."

He stands on the footpath and watches her car lights disappear. It is beginning to rain, a light patter. Across the road is his brother's car, his old home, their tree hideout, so many abandoned things. He feels utterly washed out. He shoves his hands into his pockets and sets off. He'll walk around Mayton for a while, walk off the stress of the job, see if he can settle his thoughts.

Within an hour he is back in the lane, gazing at the cottage. Is it stalking, if he sits on her porch to be near her? He decides it probably is. He walks to the end of the lane and sits by her fence instead, his back against her gate. The earth is cold and damp, the timbers wet, but he doesn't care.

From here, Johnny can see the lights of the Station, the fire tower, the crooked rows of rain-slick cobbles marching down to Main Street. There, a yellow streetlight stands sentry. The fuschia bushes he planted last spring are tossing in the breeze, their dancing leaves shimmering silver then dark in the wash of light from the Station.

He leans his head against the palings. He likes it here, near Quinn. He cannot stay forever, but tonight he'll steal this fragment of peace.

Inside, Clyde sits up on his blanket and whines. Quinn stirs, murmurs something and goes back to sleep. Clyde watches the door for a while, his ears pricked and his tail wagging. Inexplicably, Johnny stays outside. He is close, Clyde knows, all his focus upon them, but he does not come in.

Clyde grows weary of waiting and lies down again to sleep.

Chapter 16

Johnny is a hero. He has saved three lives and prevented a huge tragedy for the town. Everyone in the community wants to shake his hand. But he is uncomfortable with the praise, acutely aware of the desolation of the young man's family. He keeps his head down, works hard and avoids people. Even Quinn.

Sad, when anything dies. He frowns. Any*one*.

Attending the drowned man's funeral is excruciating. Through all the hymns, the Eucharistic Prayer and eulogies, Johnny stands at the rear of the church, hunched against his memories. Thea and Grant are on duty so Sarah has come with him, but her eyes are filled with her own tears, and her hand on his arm is shaking. He slips his arm around her and she sobs into his shoulder, but his heart is wrapped in frozen silence. As soon as he can, with all possible politeness, he escapes.

I am checking methodically through the design for a manor house restoration when I hear the solemn toll of the church bells. I pause over the bathroom plan. Clyde is in the garden, and Doris is watching TV in the next room.

"I wonder," I tell the clients' proposed marble vanity, "if the fire crew are at the funeral?" Johnny, specifically. I've heard about the rescue from Lollie. I am haunted by the fate of the car driver and my heart goes out to the crew. It must have been devastating for the people who had to stand by, unable to help. I can't imagine how Johnny feels, and I haven't seen him to ask.

This afternoon, Doris and I have our appointment with the lawyer. I help her up the steep, narrow steps into his office, and just as we get in, my phone rings. It is Az. I have no time to chat so I ignore her call and bring a seat forward for Doris.

Hemi shuffles some papers on the glass-covered guitar amp he uses as a coffee table. "This is an unusual situation, Doris. You have been in a relationship with Alfred for a decade, so you are certainly entitled to his assets. Are you sure you don't want the cottage?"

"I don't want it," she says emphatically. "I'd like to give it to Quinn, and live there with her until I die. Then Quinn can inherit it from me." She looks pleased with her plan. I feel like a cad for wanting to abandon her.

"What do you think about that arrangement, Quinn?"

"I have a business designing luxury homes around the world, it is difficult for me to commit to being in Mayton fulltime, or for the long term..."

"It won't be too long term," pipes Doris. "I'm ninety-two!"

"Don't be depressing," I snap.

"I'm being realistic."

"Well, I'm being realistic when I say I'm not sure I can stay with you, making English Breakfast tea and toast every morning for the duration. I have my own life and a business to run!" The instant the words come out, I am sorry. Doris looks shocked, as though she hadn't realised she was a burden.

I am just as shocked to realise she's not one. I *like* living with Doris. It is nuts but it's true. I think how hard Az would laugh if she heard me say that. I bite my lip. "I'm so sorry, Doris."

"I know I'm a burden."

"You're not. I spoke without thinking and I apologise." I feel terrible.

"You are a very impetuous young lady."

"Yes." I imagine that Doris and my mother would enjoy comparing notes.

She lifts her chin. "But we will sell the house and split the proceeds."

"Doris! You should take all the money. What is Alfred's is yours."

"I don't want all the money," she insists. "Alfred would want you to have something."

"Grumps wanted me to provide for you, and anyway I have his dog."

"You are welcome to it! That animal is messy and noisy and he..."

"Ladies, please." Hemi holds up his hands. His eyes are on me. "Do you think there might be a path you could take that lies between the extremes of selling or staying?"

Beside me, Doris is shaking. I take her hand and she grips it hard. "No." Yes. What am I thinking? I don't want to stay in Mayton. I don't want to leave, either.

Hemi is still watching me. "I can arrange the legal paperwork for you, Doris, and put you in touch with a local realtor. But I wonder if you are both being a bit hasty in your decision? Perhaps give it a week or two to think about it, then discuss things between you."

My brows go up. "Is this your professional advice as a lawyer?"

Hemi taps his teeth with his fountain pen. "My wife Rae is a very kind person, and she has been worried about Doris. Just last week, Rae said how happy she is that Doris has you for company, and to help her now Alfred is gone." He twinkles. "I want Rae to be happy. For that, I need Doris to be happy."

I feel like I've stepped into a soap drama. What do *I* need? Is anyone asking?

But there is no need to ask, I know. I need Johnny. And I haven't seen him all week.

Preparations for the parade have kept Johnny busy, as it's now barely a week away. Every day after work, he rides down to Rosa's to check on Mamma and take any supplies they need. Mamma is slowly coming good, and Rosa looks tired but happy.

As he finishes up on Friday, his aunt follows him down the stairs. "Between you and me, I think hospital was good for your mamma. She saw people in there in a far worse state than her. Praise be, she is now eating better, and even spoke this morning of going to see Stella."

"Is she well enough to come home?" It has been nagging at Johnny that their old house is empty. Seeing Quinn again feels miraculous and has made him restless.

"She says *No*, amore." Rosa comes close, cups his face in her workworn hands. "Giulia will never go back to Mayton to live, Johnny. To Italy, yes. A few months' visit, perhaps more." Her eyes are sad but she is smiling.

Johnny can see nothing to smile at. He hugs Rosa. "It will be good for you both to see Zia Stella. I'll send money for your tickets."

"I will pay it, tesoro," Rosa protests. Johnny shakes his head, pulls on his helmet and kicks back the stand. The guttural roar of the bike drowns any argument. He clasps her hand briefly, nods farewell and rides home through the winter drizzle.

Johnny has always been sure Mamma would come home. She has friends who still ask about her when they see Johnny in the street – Giulia's tennis buddies, her quilting group, the fundraising ladies at church. Mamma's house has been waiting for her, waiting until she regained strength enough to come home and embrace all the memories and love. Her husband's things are there, and Mario's things, waiting for her untouched, just as she instructed Johnny when she left.

Johnny has been the guardian of those things. Lately, he feels they are becoming a burden.

As he turns into Fire Station Lane, he almost runs over Clyde. The dog scoots into the fuschias, then follows him into the yard. "You need to go home." Johnny peels off his jacket while Clyde lolls happily at him. "I worry. One day you will be flattened by the fire truck and Quinn will blame me."

Quinn. Her name brings a hollow ache to his heart and his loins. He is not sure which is most disturbing. He doesn't have much time to decide though, because Quinn darts into the yard. She is still wearing her running gear, had been warming down when she heard the bike come in.

"Johnny! It's been ages. How's your mamma, is she getting better? Did you get the steam pump going?" She sparkles at him in the gathering dusk. "Thea said you went to the funeral. Are you OK?"

How to answer that? Johnny shakes out his hair, damp from the rain. He stows his helmet on his bike and his boots in the porch. He isn't OK but he can't express why. Around town, Johnny Best is a hero. Within, he is struggling with loss all over again. "Clyde was in the lane. I nearly ran him over." He doesn't know why this bothers him. Clyde is always in the lane. Johnny is always nearly running him over.

Quinn looks into his midnight gaze. "I'm sorry."

"It's not your fault, it's just Clyde, he..."

"I don't mean about that." She stands on tiptoes, hugs him and rests her head on his chest. Johnny means to resist her, keep her at arm's length, but she feels so good he can't help it. He wraps her in his arms. For a long time they stand like this, breathing, two heartbeats melding into one.

Johnny sighs, and his breath ruffles her hair. *This woman is incredible. I don't deserve her.*

"Come home with me, Johnny."

"I can't, I..."

"It's not a suggestion." She takes his hand in hers, calling for Clyde to come. The dog runs in from the shadows to lead the way.

"Quinn, you deserve so much more, I don't think..."

"What are you talking about?"

Johnny looks at her. Hazel eyes shot with gold, reflecting the glow of the streetlamp. Light blonde hair frosted with raindrops. He hesitates.

"Johnny, I've waited all week to see you. I thought I should give you space but now I'm not sure that was a good idea. I want you in my bed, is that too terrible to ask?"

He swallows his surprise, the sudden leap of desire. "No, not terrible."

"So glad," she says drily, and drags him through her picket gate.

Quinn has made her need clear, so he follows her and kisses her in the hall. She leans in. She is hot. Sparkling. Firing his blood. He stops. "What about..."

"Doris? Asleep. She won't wake 'til at least midnight." She grins. "As long as we're quiet. Ish."

"Ish?" His voice is husky.

"I'm leaning towards 'ish' because I'm not sure I can be totally..." A yelp of surprise turns into laughter as Johnny sweeps her off her feet and into her room. He nudges the door shut against Clyde.

"OK, bella." He shrugs off his clothes and kisses her rain-cold lips, slips his hand inside her tee. She does a cute little wriggle and sheds it, then undoes her bra. He kisses her shoulder, absorbing the cinnamon scent of her. "Bellissima. You are so beautiful."

She kicks off her knickers, stretches naked beneath his smouldering gaze. He feels his blood surge. What a woman. He uses gentle hands to trace whorls of fire. Throat, clavicle, shoulder, rib and glorious rounded hip, he kisses each in turn. Hard work to hold himself in check, but worth it. He cups her breasts, teasing her with tongue and thumb. He is enjoying her body and in no hurry, but Quinn is.

"Come here, you." She pulls him down to meet her.

When Quinn wakes, Johnny follows her into the kitchen. She chops vegetables and he stirfries them. He adds garlic, ginger and chilli sauce. A dash of honey.

He presents the pan with a flourish. "Traditional family recipe." As Quinn laughs, he switches to Italian. "*No,* I know next time I must cook Italian for you."

"It will be my pleasure to eat your Italian cooking." He knows she means it light-heartedly, but the words cast a sudden shadow.

"Not too soon. At present I live in a fire station." *I am unfit for you.*

"You can cook in this kitchen," she laughs. "After all, you painted it!"

After they eat, she shuts the dog in the kitchen and leads him back to bed. It takes all Johnny's strength to break through that shadow and show his passion for her. He is suddenly feeling inadequate. Not enough. For this woman, especially. *I should leave now, before you work out that my life is a mess and find someone better.*

Quinn seems satisfied, though. He is amazed they don't wake Doris. As she drifts to sleep again in his arms, tousled and replete, he stares at the ceiling, alone with his thoughts.

I wake to sunlight streaming in and realise I've overslept. I look lazily for Johnny, but he's not there. His shirt is still on my floor, which I take to be a good sign.

Perhaps he has gone to let Clyde out, or to make coffee. I hope it is the latter. I lie back and stretch luxuriously. I feel fabulous all over. Johnny has that effect on me.

Slowly, seeping into my review of last night's sensuous activities comes a discordant sound I associate with neither coffee nor Clyde. I wrap myself in Johnny's shirt and go to investigate.

"Ciao!" I call from my porch.

"Morning." Johnny sounds distracted. He is not speaking Italian anymore. Does that mean something?

"My fence has been broken for weeks, do you have to fix it now?"

"Yes." He is hammering fence palings like his life depends on it. Doris is sitting in the sun, watching him.

"Morning, Doris! Johnny, it's Saturday morning, let me make you breakfast."

"No, thankyou." He is frowning.

"Oo, that sounds lovely! You can make breakfast for me instead."

I look at Doris. "Surely you've had breakfast?"

"Oh yes, hours ago. But you can make me another if you like."

"Toast?" I guess, and she beams. I can't help but smile back. This fades as I switch to Johnny. "Please?"

"Sorry, I want to finish this."

I fry honey-cured bacon and eggs on toast for Doris, then go out to sit under my tree. There is a curve in the trunk which fits me perfectly if I lean against it just so. I watch as Johnny replaces the last few palings, then moves methodically along the fence making sure all the nail heads are flush. When he's finished, he puts down the hammer and stares in silence at his hands.

"Why today?" I ask.

"I need to fix the fence before..." He glances distractedly at me, gets up and puts the hammer away in the garage.

I follow, puzzled by this angst I'm seeing. I trap him between the Morris and the workbench and slide up against him. He is shirtless, blue jeans riding low on his hips. He looks incredible. "Your problem is that you think too much."

"Mario used to say that."

"You should just kiss me more."

"OK." He gathers me close and kisses me. When we come up for air he says, "You look good in my shirt."

"I feel good in your shirt, mmm *yes*, do I feel good." Johnny grins as though I'm dazzling him just by standing here. I know how he feels. I grab his hands and walk backwards, tugging him past the Morris. "Let's take Clyde for a walk and get breakfast on the way."

Gill's Hot Buns is busy with Saturday morning customers. More than a few glances are exchanged when Johnny and I walk in together. He has pulled on his rollneck jersey and I have leggings under, but I am obviously still wearing his shirt.

"I hear shirt dresses are all the rage." Billie slides past me in the queue.

"You should know," I grin.

She laughs. "Sadly, I never got an offer to wear *that* shirt dress. It looks good on you, girlfriend."

"I'm pretty happy with it."

At the counter, Gill winks at me as I collect our coffee order. She throws in a cheese twist for Clyde. Johnny is smouldering in the corner, the collie at his feet looking cute. He is attracting attention from all the weekend tourists. Several sleek, monied forty-somethings are fawning over the dog, trying to make conversation.

I drag him out before he is propositioned. "The trouble with you is you look so hot, I can't take you anywhere."

The albatross wings lift. "What can I say? Firefighters are sexy."

"They didn't *know* you were a firefighter!"

His mouth quirks. "I told them straight away. You don't need a pickup line when you have the sexiest job in the..."

"You did not, I was watching, you said barely two words to them."

"You were watching me?" Johnny wraps his arm around me, nearly squashing Clyde who is trotting between us.

I tilt my face for his kiss. "Never."

Johnny needs to check a few things at the Station, so I wait for him in the yard. I am staring idly at the fire tower, imagining how the numbers I ordered will look up there, when I realise they have not yet arrived in the post. I yelp in dismay.

"Disaster?"

"I forgot about the decorations!"

"Didn't you order them last week?"

"Yes! They said the parcel would come Tuesday. It didn't, so I rang and they said late Friday. I forgot to chase it up again." I was too busy loitering outside yesterday afternoon, waiting for you to come home...

Johnny bends to fuss over Clyde. "The post office is open 'til noon."

"I'll ring." It takes three phone calls, but I discover my parcel has been delivered by mistake to the post office in the next town.

"It's a huge consignment," the post office bloke there complains. "Thought I was gonna need a forklift to get it off the truck."

"Will it fit in the boot of a Morris Minor?"

"Shouldn't think so, love. Doesn't 'minor' mean small?"

"The Morris isn't *that* small." I gaze idly at Clyde, draped upside down over Johnny's boots. He lolls his tongue at me, and manages to lick his right eyeball. "How heavy is the parcel, exactly? Can I lift it?"

"Not unless you're a sumo wrestler. Are you a sumo wrestler?"

I look over at Johnny. "No, but I have the next best thing." I cut the call. "I hate to pivot from sexy brunch date to mundane domestic tasks, but... Come for a drive, Johnny?"

The Morris starts after a little encouragement and I back it into the lane. Johnny slides into the passenger seat.

I check, "Did you manage to shut Clyde in the house?"

"Yes. He's disappointed. He doesn't like Doris's TV programs."

"I can't bring him, I don't know how big this parcel is."

The Morris is noisy and cumbersome to drive, and Main Street has become busier since we walked down for coffee. I am glad to get out on the open road. I drive the long stretch downhill to the river and across the bridge. At the site of the car accident there are still traffic cones scattered, and a great scar in the riverbank. Johnny looks resolutely at his hands as we pass it.

"Lollie said you're a hero."

"No."

"You should be proud you saved three lives." *I'm* proud of you. "It's what you go to work every day to do, saving lives. It must be nice to be recognised for it. Imagine if you hadn't been there and everyone had gone in the river, the whole town would have..."

"Quinn." Johnny's brows knit. The message is clear. *Leave it.*

I concentrate on driving. Some part of me wants to cry. That stupid, emotional part that keeps interfering lately. I clear my throat. "Sometimes I should just keep my mouth shut." This gets the faint quirk of a smile. "I know, I know, hard to change the habit of a lifetime."

"I didn't say that." Johnny grins. He leans back and rests his arm behind me. After a moment, his fingers slide into my hair and he kisses me lightly on the cheek. Is that an apology? His voice is quiet. "We often go to car accidents. This one was bad because I couldn't save him. The deceased was the same age as Mario."

Oh, Johnny, I'm sorry. He doesn't say anything more, and somehow I manage to stave off my tears and reach the post office without causing a road incident.

The postal manager wants to talk about my vintage car, and laughs loudly when I ask for my parcel. "That huge parcel out the back is yours? It weighs a ton and you're such a wee dot, even with my help I don't think you'll be able to carry it."

"She'll be right." I beckon to Johnny and he unfolds himself from the Morris.

"Oh, I see you've brought heavy lifting equipment. Reckon you'll be right as rain."

It takes some manoeuvring, but Johnny gets the parcel into the boot. A bit of the packaging is torn, and red and white flags are poking out. I feel a buzz of excitement. The Station is going to look great!

Johnny is folding himself back into my passenger seat. "Thankyou for your help, Johnny, I couldn't have done this without you." I gaze at him. "Do you know how sexy you look in my car?"

"I have to be in your car to look sexy?"

I laugh. It is good to bask again in the glint of those midnight eyes. I start the Morris and we clatter out onto the highway. "Come back to mine and I'll show you how sexy you are everywhere."

Chapter 17

Thea and Johnny come looking for me the day before the parade. I am in my tree.

"Hellooo!" Thea yodels. "Earth to Quinn."

"It's not even eight in the morning, do you lot never sleep?"

"I'm wondering if *you* sleep in your tree," she grins.

"Not always." I drop an acorn on Johnny and he catches it deftly.

Thea says, "We're ready for your decorations to go up. What do you need?" I toss my paperback down to her, and her eyes light up. "Ooh, Lady Hatwick. Is this Kate's book? I've been meaning to get a copy."

I climb out of the tree. "You can take that one, I've read it twice already. I want it back, though."

"It looks delicious." She tucks it into her work pants.

I smile at Johnny and try to focus on Thea's question. What do I need? Apart from Johnny, that is. I haven't seen him since our post office run. "I need access to a ladder. A big one. I've got bunting to go across the front of the Station, and on the fire engine, and a big '125' to hang on the tower."

"Johnny can park the truck where you want it, you can use that ladder. We'll have to clip you in, safety first and all that." Thea gives Johnny a look I can't decipher. "You two work together on the decorations. I've tasked Grant and Sarah with setting up the marquee and trestles. And Johnny, keep an eye out for Linc, he might drop by for a final check of the old engine. He's bringing his horses first thing in the morning, and the parade kicks off at eleven. Cross fingers we've thought of everything."

Johnny stirs. "You have. It's all good."

"I'm sure it will be fine, Thea, you've done an amazing job of organising everything."

She checks her watch. "I gotta go, I have a meeting with the Council roads guys in half an hour. Meet me at four at Little Bird, I want a sitrep then from everyone. I'll buy the coffees."

Thea strides off, the bright pink Lady Hatwick novel with its steamy cover an incongruous addition to her Fire Service uniform. I hope she remembers to take it out of her pocket before her meeting at the Council chambers.

"So," I turn to Johnny and lose my train of thought beneath his quizzical gaze. "Um... The ladder. Actually, I don't care about the ladder, how about we take a quick tea break and you come inside and..."

Johnny doesn't answer, he just jingles the truck keys in his pocket and heads for the Station. Duty calls, apparently. I whistle for Clyde, lock him in so he can't get tangled in bunting or run over by the truck, and chase after Johnny. As I come up alongside, he drapes his arm over my shoulders and kisses the top of my head.

"I know," I tell him, "it was an attractive offer. You'd better hope it wasn't a one-time, last chance and we'll throw in a set of steak knives offer or you'll regret this for the rest of your life."

Johnny laughs. "Watching you climb that ladder will be the consolation prize."

It is. I am at my best climbing. I feel graceful, fearless and strong. I am in shorts too, so he can look at my legs. Johnny teaches me how to clip myself in, then supervises from below. He strings out coloured bunting from the parcel at his feet and hands it up. A couple of times he needs to move the truck to get it positioned perfectly. I jump in for a ride and try all the switches, asking in turn what each one does until he swats me with a clipboard.

I love being up on the ladder. When I've finished stringing bunting along the front of the Station, we move to the tower. Johnny extends the ladder its full length. I am high enough that I can see all of Mayton below. There is my little cottage, and Main Street, and Johnny's family villa. Olive's bookshop in its courtyard. The wide sweep of the river, the park, the cemetery, and blue-shaded mountains in the distance. "I have to say, it's better being on the ladder in daylight."

"Take good note of that," says Johnny.

"I think I can see Wellington!"

"You can't see Wellington. It's only a seventeen-metre ladder."

"It is absolutely Wellington." I haul up the number '1' using the pulley Johnny has rigged up, and lean to fix it to the wall. The tower is rustic stonework so I am using a drill with a masonry bit. "Why do you have a ladder anyway? There are no highrise buildings in Mayton."

"The Mayton Hotel is three storeys." I lift an eyebrow and he says, "I know, rural trucks don't usually have ladders. There was some kind of paperwork mix up, and our new truck came with one. Or perhaps Thea was just very persuasive." He grins. "I find it's great for getting things out of trees."

"What sort of things?" I am grinning now, too.

"Oh, you know. Cats."

"Do you often get called out to rescue cats?"

"Never. But you know, I got a call recently to rescue Billie and her friend from a tree."

"I'm not surprised, if Billie was involved. I hear her friend is usually very competent." I lean back to look at the '1'. "Does that look straight?"

"Close enough."

"What does that mean, is it crooked?"

"Quinn, it looks great."

"Don't do that to me. Tell me it's straight."

"It's good. Straight as." He crosses himself.

"OK, send up the '2'."

We work hard until a quarter to four and get all the decorations up. I stand in the road to view our handiwork. Red and white flags are strung over the Station's brick frontage and the truck is festooned. In the yard behind, Sarah and Grant's marquee looks very smart and inviting. Above all, the soot-blackened fire tower declares in bright, bold numbers that the Station is '125'. I tell myself the '1' is *not* a little crooked. As Johnny said, it's good.

"Great work, team!" Sarah fist-bumps Grant and Johnny, and hugs me. "Tomorrow is going to be fun."

I feel an unaccustomed glow. Everything is coming together. Tomorrow the horses will arrive, the vehicles will form up, and the whole town will come together to celebrate. Maybe some good stuff really does happen in Mayton.

"Thea said four o' clock." Johnny hauls down the big roller door, slides the locks into place.

"Have you put the phone through to Olive?" Sarah checks.

"Yes."

At this, she, Grant and Johnny walk away down Main Street. I follow, laughing. "You mean someone will ring the Station for an emergency and get Olive's bookshop?"

Sarah grins at me. "The Prime Minister rang once. She was on the election trail and wanted to visit. Olive sold her a war history omnibus and the full Women in Leadership collection before she could get through to us."

I fall in alongside Johnny. As we walk, our arms brush. I wrap my fingers in his and felt his quick, light squeeze in response. The latent power of this huge, gentle man leaves me tingling. I know I am being sentimental. I remind myself that men are unreliable, I will soon become boring and then he will cheat on me. I should move on and find a new tree.

There is a little part of me that knows Johnny wouldn't cheat. That he couldn't be dishonest if he tried. And that little part is becoming more vocal.

Johnny seems comfortable with my hand in his, so we walk into the bookshop like that. Olive raises an eyebrow, Kate gives me a wink, and soon the five of us are chatting comfortably over coffees in the Children's Corner.

Thea comes in at two minutes past four, apologising. Sarah makes shushing noises and pushes a tiny chair towards her. Kate hands her a cappuccino.

"Are the decorations up?" she asks me.

"Yes, cap'n."

Thea looks round the group. "The trestles and the marquee?"

Sarah salutes. "Aye, sir ma'am boss."

"Johnny, how's the steam pump and the handcart?"

"All present and correct." Johnny eases back in his beanbag – he is far too big for the little kids' chairs – and raises his mug lazily.

Thea frowns. "Grant, did you ring around to check all the old trucks are coming?"

"Thea, it's all done. Relax."

She notices Kate at last. "Do you and Linc have a plan for the morning?"

"We'll bring the horses in at dawn – well, Linc will, I'll be asleep! We'll plait up and be at yours by eight. Linc wants to give the horses a quick practice pulling the engine, then he'll rest them until the parade at eleven. Can we turn them out in the stationyard?"

"Yes. It'll save Johnny mowing the lawn."

"Thankyou," he says drily.

"Do you think there'll be any problems pulling the engine?"

Kate smiles at Thea. "The horses should be fine. They are comfortable pulling anything round the farm. And they go brilliantly in the landau, even with big trucks passing."

Olive agrees. "They are well-trained. Linc wouldn't bring them if he thought it was unsafe."

Thea allows herself a quick smile. "Well, then, I can't think of anything else. Good work, everyone."

Olive throws a teatowel at her. "Now you are banned from mentioning the parade for at least fifteen minutes. Tell me, how many of you have read Kate's book?"

Grant and Sarah yell together, "Ooh, we have!" And I catch Kate's eye with a grin. She buries her face in her hands, her cheeks flaming.

Olive is ruthless. "If you can't handle the heat, Kate, get out of the kitchen. Or the gutter, or the bedroom or something." She turns her attention to Sarah. "What did you think of Lady Hatwick's argument with Lord Tennsdale? Is she a spiteful shrew, or a budding suffragette ahead of her time?"

Linc arrives first thing in the morning, riding Dash and leading Waiata. I hear hooves clattering in the lane and run out to see. I run back in and get Doris and Clyde. Clyde leaps at the horses, barking, so I run back again to put him away.

Johnny is in the stationyard. "Morning."

Linc nods across the yard. "The steam pump's looking great. Is the tank still empty?"

"Yes."

"Good. My horses are not the heavy draught type that'd normally tow this engine. We don't want the extra weight of water."

They study the old engine. It sits squarely on four wheels, its timbers freshly oiled and brasses polished. The rear wheels are larger than the front, and the steam pump paraphernalia is mounted on a wagon bed, with a long pole out front for the horses.

I jog into the yard and Johnny raises an eyebrow. I know my turquoise poncho is somewhat extra, but it looks fabulous with my indigo jeans. I twinkle at him and slide under his arm. Linc is studiously not looking at us, with something that is definitely not a grin if you asked him.

Johnny clears his throat. "If we push this thing into the lane, you'll have more room to harness up."

"Good idea." Linc ties his horses to several rings in the stationyard wall, probably installed many years ago for that exact purpose. He puts his shoulder to the back left wheel of the steam pump.

"I'll help." I run to the other wheel.

Johnny lifts the central pole. "Ready, push." A pause. "Quinn, push your side."

"I am pushing!"

Johnny looks at Linc, then at me. "Come up here and steer instead. I'll push your wheel." This is more successful, and we soon get the steam pump through the gateway. Manoeuvring under Johnny's quiet direction, we turn it around in the lane.

At that moment, Kate arrives in a Holden ute. She has Sue, her camera and a Labrador dog in tow. While Sue and the dog go to look for a good vantage point in the lane, Kate begins to drag the harness from the tray.

I help her. "I know some people have a thing for chains and leather, but this is excessive." Kate laughs and tells me to lift my end, and between us we get the harness laid out and organised, a set for each horse.

Linc comes and swaps the collars because we mixed them up, fits the harness to the horses and exchanges their halters for driving bridles. He gathers up the long reins, walks the horses into the lane and backs them, one horse either side of the pole. The grey horse swings sideways and steps over the pole, so Linc takes them through it all again. "Back, Dash. Waiata, back. Waiata, over. Alright, whoa."

Johnny lifts the pole so Linc can fasten the straps. Waiata stamps and tosses his head, anxious to be off. Johnny puts a steadying hand to his bridle.

Gathering the reins, Linc says, "They haven't pulled this before, but it's not much heavier than the landau with people in. We'll see how it goes." He nods to Johnny to release the grey. "OK, guys, walk up."

I watch, fascinated, as the horses move forward together. They feel the extra weight, hear the deep rumble of the iron wheels, and hesitate. A soothing click and a "Move up" from Linc brings them back on task and they stride confidently down the lane.

The horse-drawn engine is on the move! Sue is clicking photos and I'm fizzing, I can't help myself. I run along behind the horses like I'm four years old.

Linc turns right at Main Street and drives down as far as Little Bird Bookshop. Olive is waving wildly out her coffee window. With a squeal of wheels and clatter of hooves, Linc turns the steam pump in the street. Kate's sister Lori is in the courtyard with her three boys, and they dart forward at the sight of the engine. We run along together as the horses trot majestically back to the Station.

"Fire, fire!" Nikau yells, waving his arms behind the engine.

Taika joins in, "Get da water quick, all-a world is on fire. Run, Yinc, run!"

The horses pull up next to Kate and Thea, right under the fluttering flags. Linc tips his chin at Kate. "Hey, beautiful, can you grab Taika before he's flung into next week? Waiata doesn't like little boys hanging on his bridle."

Kate scoops up her nephew. "Taika, go and play with Brick. He might be getting bored, sitting there while auntie Sue takes pictures." The boys dash off to plague the Labrador, and Kate reaches for Linc's hand. "You look gorgeous, darling, and the horses are doing a wonderful job. What a great idea, Thea!"

She grins. "Not mine. It's Quinn who thought of getting horses for the steam pump engine. And thanks to you two, it's all coming together."

I am buzzing with delight. "It is my family's ink sketch coming to life! So cool."

Sue is snapping photos of the steam pump parked beside the modern fire engine. "The old and the new! Brilliant. Linc, do try to look more serious and professional. You are grinning like a Cheshire cat."

We could have stood round admiring the horses in the steam pump all day, but Linc wants to give them a rest. He unharnesses Dash and Waiata and turns them loose to graze. Johnny clears a small mountain of pavers from against the stationyard wall and manages to shut the heavy old gate behind them.

With a rattle and a bump, a little green car hurtles into the lane, driving over three fuschia bushes and scraping a fender on Lollie's fence. Olive wriggles out of the car with a tray of compostable cups. "Coffee, anyone?" She taps the lids in turn. "Long black, flat white, another flat white, cappuccino. And there's another tray in the car."

Sue leads the charge. "Olive, you're a lifesaver."

Kate sips her flat white. "You've closed the shop?"

"Yes, you've abandoned me today so I've given up," Olive grins. "Actually, I'd rather be here with the horses anyway. What did you think of the trial run, Linc?"

The discussion pivots to horses, and I turn my attention to Johnny. He is standing at the end of the lane, coffee in hand, staring in the direction of his old house.

"A penny for your thoughts?" I nudge him and get a grunt in reply. "You know, I think we should get married and move in with my seventeen ex-boyfriends and eleven kids."

He looks at me absently. "Pardon?"

"Never mind." I get the feeling that today, even with all this bustle and excitement, even while Johnny is lifting and helping, dragging and organising, only half of him is here.

Chapter 18

Doris and I get ready for the parade together. I lend her my lip gloss and a shawl, and she helps me make a fruit platter for Lollie. Shirley arrives and we chatter our way down to Lollie's gate. Adam has set a table and chairs on their front lawn for a fine, head-on view of the parade as it makes its way down Main Street. They'll be front row for its arrival at the Fire Station.

Lollie is enjoying herself hugely. Like Doris, she loves fire trucks and men in uniform and they are everywhere in Mayton this morning. She encourages Shirley and Doris in their wicked observations and soon the three of them are in stitches. Adam brings out a big bowl of punch and Lollie starts ladling it into glasses.

I sniff at it suspiciously and Lollie laughs, "It's non-alcoholic."

"Yeah, right."

"Well, I added just a splash of champagne..."

I turn to Adam. "How bad is it? Will Doris be drunk under the table by lunchtime?"

He grins. "Don't worry, it'll be fine."

I waggle a finger at my step-grandmother. "Behave. I'll be back soon."

"Never. You go away and enjoy your yummy fireman."

"Doris!"

She tells Shirley in not so *sotto voce*, "Do you know she has a fireman? That lovely, tall young fellow who likes to paint things." I make good my escape.

Johnny and his crew are with the truck at the other end of Main Street, ready to join the parade. Linc and his horses will lead everyone. I give Dash a quick pat and exchange a grin with Johnny. Leaning on the step of his truck, he looks confident and professional. Gotta love a man in uniform, I think, then shake myself for sounding like Doris.

I wander down the parade line towards the river. Here is the enthusiastic gaggle of schoolchildren who will follow the horses, carrying fire buckets. There's been some attempt to outfit them in period costumes. Here is the ragtag bunch of vintage fire trucks and their even more ragtag drivers, with strict instructions to stay behind Johnny's truck to avoid running into horses and children. Here are the various emergency vehicles, including Mayton's ambulance and, rather obscurely, the town mayor in full regalia in a Mercedes convertible. Here is the brass band from Wellington, who came even though Thea tried to stop them. If there's a procession, they're into it. The whole shebang is bookended by police cars.

The cold wind brings a flurry of autumn leaves from the park. I check the sky. According to the Bureau, it is not supposed to rain, but this is New Zealand so it might rain anyway. Or hail, for some variety.

Shrugging deeper into my jacket I watch the higgeldy line of people and vehicles, the stamping horses. The entire length of Main Street is lined with the entire populace of Mayton –

everyone from the district, I swear – waiting to see the parade. I am overwhelmed by a sudden, ridiculous sense of pride. I know this is a team effort and it's all Thea's organising, but the original idea was mine. And I'm proud of it. To have this parade laid out before me in all its colourful, semi-historically-accurate glory is fantastic. What a thing. Grumps would have loved it.

As a police siren blips the pre-arranged start signal and Linc clicks to his horses, I wonder if Doris is thinking about Grumps, too. Johnny's truck moves off, and I jog through the park to get ahead of the procession. I want to see him arrive at the Fire Station.

Halfway through the rose garden I run straight into José.

"What the..?" It is definitely José. In his Savile Row suit, Montblanc cufflinks and suede loafers, it is without a doubt my ex-boyfriend from Barcelona. My cheating ex. In Mayton, of all places.

He gives me a wide smile. "Quinn, darling."

"What the hell are you doing here?"

"I'm with Asmita."

"Az is here, too?"

"If you mean Asmita, your friend from Auckland, yes. She is looking for coffee. Naturally, this is how I found you. I told her we've had some miscommunication lately and she offered to help. She has been very kind."

"There's been no miscommunication. I blocked you. Then I moved back to New Zealand."

José spreads his hands. "See? Why would you do a thing like that unless it was a terrible miscommunication? I love you, my darling. I made a little mistake, I admit, but you know it is all water under the bridge."

"You mean now your new girlfriend has left you, too, and you need me to wash your socks and be nice to your father so you don't have to."

"No, no, I have a housekeeper who washes my socks. She is very good with socks. I want you to come back to me because you are the most beautiful woman in the world and it is only I who can make you happy."

"I am happy here." I am surprised to discover it's true. Today, with Johnny and Thea and Kate and Linc and Olive and those two crazy little boys and the beautiful horses, I am happy. I look more closely at José. Under all his cajoling, he looks nervous. The faint tic, the unconscious tug at his shirtcuffs, I know him too well. "You've landed the Olympic contract!" I say accusingly.

"Quinn, my dearest love, this has nothing to do with..."

"You've got the contract to build the next Olympic village and your father knows you can't do the job. He needs me, and that's why you're here."

José takes my hand and presses it to his lips. "It is true I can offer you your job straight back with my father's firm, on twice the salary and a new car. El padre said also he will buy us a better apartment, because after all you will need a bigger office..." He flashes a smile, runs his thumb tenderly over my wrist. "All that has nothing to do with me being here. I am in love with you. Why else would I follow you right across the world to this... this...?" He waves his hand at Main Street, the cheering little crowd and the parade, as though he's at a loss. His handsome face looks pained.

"My point exactly, José. Why else? I know you'd happily replace me in the blink of an eye with your housekeeper, your chauffer, your candlestickmaker, and never think to look back. But your father cannot replace me. You go home and tell José Senior that I know my worth and I have no interest in working for him again. I also have no interest in you. Goodbye." I pull away, ignoring his protestations, and flee through the park.

Across the road, I can see Az banging on the door of Gill's Hot Buns – closed today, like everything else – but I do not stop for her. Instead I duck into Johnny's backyard, brush through the carob hideout and that hot, red car, and cross the road to join Doris and Lollie and their party in Fire Station Lane.

No one notices me arrive. They are watching Linc's horses make a magnificent turn, right in front of the Fire Station. The kaikaranga calls them in and a group of college students perform a rousing haka pōwhiri to welcome the parade. The horses pull up beneath the bunting, Johnny's truck rolls in, and a thousand people cheer. Thea makes a speech, followed by the mayor who makes a longer one. Then Gill rolls out a massive cake. Taika, Nikau and all the school children rush to get a plate.

Lollie's group also go looking for cake. I hang back on the edge of the crowd. I don't want to see Az, and I definitely don't want to see José. I'd like to see Johnny, but he's just about the only person I can't see. Anywhere. I hope that soon he'll find me.

After a long, disappointing wait, no Johnny and no cake, I go home.

Johnny has the truck crawling along nicely, taking care not to run over any schoolchildren or rear end the horses. There are sirens blipping, lights flashing, children laughing and exclaiming, and that great brass band making a hellish racket behind him. He's got to admit, after weeks of work by more than half the population of Mayton, Thea and Quinn's parade is a success. The Fire Station is turning 125 in style.

The '1' on the tower is still crooked, but no one seems to care.

Partway along Main Street, he sees Quinn's distinctive figure in her bright poncho jogging through the park. He hopes she will come to meet him at the Station, he hasn't had much time for her this week. It was nice that she came to the truck to see him before the procession started...

Hang on, who's the guy? A sharp-dressed man, wavy hair, white teeth. Handsome and debonair, styled so far out of Mayton's league that we've not only dropped the ball here but it's disintegrated. Definitely not a local. If he had to take a punt, he'd guess Spanish.

And there's the rub.

It doesn't take the smart suit kissing Quinn's hand for Johnny to read his future in bold black capitals. He should have known this was coming. Actually, he did know. He has let Quinn coax him out of his black self-doubt so he could bask in her sunshine for a little while but he knew it could never last.

What could a beautiful, intelligent, capable, sexy woman like Quinn Walker ever see in Johnny Best?

The Spanish ex is back. Johnny knows that Mario is laughing himself silly over this one. He parks his truck behind Linc, smiles for the official photos, and as soon as possible he gets the hell out of there.

He doesn't just leave the event, he leaves town. In all the fuss, no one hears his Harley start up, and a few hours out on the highway with the throttle wide open is just what he needs to clear his head.

He's not sure what can ever heal his heart.

Chapter 19

I don't know why I go to Auckland after the parade – it just brings me closer to Az, who I have not yet forgiven, and straight to my mother's doorstep because I have nowhere else to stay.

I should have planned this better. But how do you plan when your teenage crush summer boyfriend of twelve years ago turns up, sets you on fire body and soul, then leaves town and doesn't explain why? I wait three days in Mayton for Johnny. I cry three days for Johnny. And if that sounds ridiculous on paper, that's because it is. What intelligent, capable, well-travelled, financially-independent 27-year-old with her own architecture firm spends three days crying over a man?

I don't hear from Johnny at all, and even Thea can't tell me where he's gone. Yes, on Day 3, I get desperate enough to ring her. She says he's alive because he replied to her congratulatory message about the Commemoration, but she hasn't seen him. He must have gone for a ride because his bike's not here.

Riding for three days? Eventually I decide all this moping is driving me nuts, I need a change of scene. So, I leave town too.

I take Clyde, so Doris doesn't have to deal with him, a train then a plane to Auckland. They don't like dogs on trains here, but I was crying so hard and I looked so terrible, when I said he was my therapy dog they believed me.

I tell myself I've always planned to leave Mayton anyway. But this doesn't make me feel better.

Johnny turns up back in Mayton for his next rostered duty. Thea is unsure where he's living – certainly not at the Station – and Grant goes home shaking his head.

Sarah pops in to tell Thea she's worried. "I mean it. There's something wrong with Johnny. He backed the truck into a door pillar today. Broke a tail-light and damaged the concrete."

"He looks alright."

"He burnt the coffee this morning. He never does that. And he didn't say anything at the First Aid refresher."

Thea shrugs. "He never talks at those things."

"That's true. But Thea..."

"I know." She frowns. "If Johnny can't drive, something's up. Has anyone seen Quinn lately?"

In Auckland, I sleep badly for the tenth night in a row, and drag myself out to the living room.

Scarlett is on her yoga mat, lean and graceful, stretching like a cat in the sun. "Morning, honey. Join me?"

"Yoga is too slow. I'll go for a run."

"Yoga is just what you need, actually."

"You don't know what I need."

"I do, I'm your mother." Scarlett stretches majestically. "I think you need to get out and find a man. A good bonk will do wonders for that mood of yours."

"Mum!" I flop onto the couch, toying idly with Clyde's ears. "You may be right but I can't. There's someone I can't stop thinking about and I don't know why."

Scarlett arches her left foot over her head, does something seemingly impossible with her hips and her right arm. "He must be something special to tie *you* down. Handsome?"

"Jeeze, you can't imagine. He's Italian."

"Fabulous. Does this lovely Adonis have a name?"

"Johnny Best."

"Doctor? Lawyer? CEO of a healthfood company?" Scarlett looks hopeful.

"Fire fighter."

"Ooh, fit then. Brave. Wears a uniform. Gotta love a man in uniform."

"Mum, be serious!"

Scarlett sits up on her yoga mat to give me her blue-eyed, undivided attention. "What's the problem, Quinnie? You are carrying around a black cloud and I am exhausted by it."

"You are? Try living under it." I puff out my cheeks. "I don't know. Johnny seems so lost. Then he comes good, and he's amazing, then he goes all distant again. His brother died and he blames himself. He is all over the place, I don't know how to fix him."

"Why are you trying to fix him, honey? It all sounds very romantic. Just like Captain Benwick."

I wrack my memory. "From... Persuasion?"

"Exactly."

"But that's just a story!"

"Excuse you. It's *Jane Austen*. Don't try to fix him, Quinnie, just love him."

I roll my eyes. "You make it sound easy."

Scarlett gives an airy wave. "It is easy. Love makes the world go round. Look at Clyde! He loves you no matter how up and down you are. You've been moping all over the place, so this Johnny fellow must mean something to you. Just take him as he is and love him."

I snort. I stare at the ceiling. Then I stare hard at Scarlett. "You think?"

"I know." She knots her graceful limbs in a regal, equally impossible new pose. "Love him. From what you say, he needs that more than you know."

I shut my eyes. "Why couldn't you tell me this over the phone? Why did I have to come all the way up here and live in your city apartment with Alfred's hyperactive dog and eat your terrible cooking for ten whole days before you finally go all relationship guru on me?"

"Honey, you didn't ask. And my cooking is fabulous."

"You're right, I didn't. And it is *so* not."

Scarlett laughs, her earrings jangling. I glare at her for a moment, then burst into laughter too. Clyde pirouettes around us, barking.

"Takeaway tonight?" she suggests. "My old high school friend owns a glorious Chinese restaurant just down the road."

"You wait all this time to tell me that, too?"

"Homecooked meals are so much better for you."

"There are exceptions, mother dear. Your pasta would qualify as a torture device."

"You are a cross and ungrateful child."

It is one thing to know Johnny just needs love, quite another for me to work out what to do about it. I am unsure why he's gone quiet and disappeared. I don't think it could be anything Doris said because he has enormous patience and tolerance and would be unlikely to take offence at her. And it's not due to José turning up because Johnny didn't meet him.

Thankfully, I've had radio silence from José too. I push aside any thoughts of Az. I need a little break before I rekindle that friendship.

Do I want to go back to Mayton? At the beginning of autumn, I'd have said no way, never. But now... To help me think, I strip back the bedhead in the guest bedroom – it is an ugly green – and repaint it in a gorgeous yellow. I am no nearer to clarity when it's done, so I flop down on the bed and brainstorm with Clyde.

Scarlett keeps an exercise ball in the room, a big silver one. I bounce this around while he chases it and I talk to myself. "Relationship advice is all well and good, Clyde, but I don't actually *have* a relationship to be advised on." Bounce. Oof.

"He hasn't even asked where I am." Bounce. Oof.

"Does it count as a thing if you don't talk to each other?" Bounce. Oof.

"Don't look at me like that, you are a dog. Life is simple for you. I am not texting or calling him again until he calls me first." Bounce. Oops, that hit the window, aim a bit further to the right.

"If Johnny doesn't contact me, does that mean he hates me? I don't even know what went wrong." Bounce. My suitcase tumbles off the top shelf and Clyde leaps away.

When the suitcase doesn't move again, Clyde trots back to inspect it. He whines, and begins scrabbling at its pearly shell.

"Stop digging, you'll wreck my case. There's nothing in there for you!"

Clyde keeps scrabbling, his claws raking the shiny surface. I pick the case up and shake it. "See? Nothing! No food, no chew toys, stop hassling. Leave it alone!" Out falls the blue sports bra I've been unable to find since I got here – and a shirt. It is Johnny's shirt. The one I wore to the bakery that day. I freeze. How did I not see it before?

Clyde sniffs Johnny's shirt. He paws at it, then nudges it over his head. He lies there, gazing up at me, the shirt on his head like a shawl.

I try to explain. "You need to understand, things are different now." Why that is, I have no idea. The collie doesn't move. He just rolls one eye to look at me. "He doesn't hate you. He likes dogs." I don't know if he likes me. I *thought* he did. But I've made that mistake before.

Clyde stays under the shirt. He begins idly chewing the tag. "You're right. Being here is driving us both crazy. We need to go home. *I* need to go home. I miss our cottage, I miss my oak tree, I want to go to Café Diva on Friday nights. I know *you* miss running in the lane. My love life is a disaster, but I think we need to go home." Clyde rips off the tag, flips up the shawl and comes to put his head on my knee. "You agree? Good. Let's have one last run on the beach and fly out Friday."

I go straight online and book tickets before I can lose my nerve. *Please, just no one mention Johnny.* How can I go back to Mayton and not hear Johnny's name? Or see him in the street? Perhaps he has moved away. Yes, maybe all this radio silence means he's moved away. To Italy perhaps, I know he has relatives there. Or Greenland. Somewhere far away so he won't have to run into me.

Just as I close the screen, my phone pings. It is a message from Kate. *Hi. Been a while. Hope you're OK.* "I don't believe it, Clyde. She must be psychic." Rather than text a reply, I ring her.

"Quinn!" Her voice is warm. "So good to hear from you. How are you?"

"Fine. I'm in Auckland."

"Oh. Cool. We hadn't seen you around, so..."

"I'm flying into Wellington on Friday morning. I think I need to come... home." Near enough. I'm not feeling at home in Auckland anymore.

"I'm glad. Would you like me to pick you up?"

"No, thanks. I'll find my own way."

"OK, but come and have dinner with Linc and I when you've settled in."

"Thankyou." I feel the glow of her friendship.

"Will we see you at Café Diva?"

"I don't think so, sorry. Not this week."

"Fine. Linc and I will see you next week for dinner then. Bring Clyde." A pause. "You are bringing Clyde, aren't you?"

"Of course! He's the one telling me to come home."

Chapter 20

When I arrive in Wellington, I collect my suitcase from the carousel with no thought of meeting anyone. I'll catch a taxi to the freight building to pick up Clyde, then on to the train station. But as I step outside into a brisk breeze straight off the Southern Ocean, I am accosted by a familiar voice. "Going my way, babe?"

"Lollie!" I feel like I haven't seen her in a million years.

"Don't cry, doll, life is too short." Lollie is smiling through the window of Milly Molly Mandy, parked with her engine running. "Kate told me you were coming, so I thought I'd drive down to pick you up."

"Because you missed me and you're such a nice person?"

"No, because I want all the goss. Hop in." I shove my case into the back, jump in and give Lollie a hug. She laughs. "That's enough of the mushy stuff, what have you done with Clyde?"

I direct her to the pet freight building. Clyde is so ecstatic to see us, he catapults me into the rose bushes by the car and I scramble out, swearing. "Not again, Clyde, seriously. I'll post you straight back to Scarlett."

"How did he go in the Big Smoke, Quinn? Apartment life must have been interesting."

"He drove me crazy – always whining at the front door to go out, harassing cats all over the neighbourhood, following me around and scratching at the bathroom door. He was so bored, he was impossible. Never again."

"I suppose he is used to roaming free-range in Fire Station Lane and going to see Thea and Johnny whenever he wants." Lollie gives me a searching look. "Have you talked to Johnny lately?"

"I can't, Lollie. He hasn't replied to my messages so what can I say?"

"Oh, I don't know, something like 'You are the most gorgeous man on the planet, I think about you all the time, I want to rip your clothes off and have my wicked way with you right here on the...'"

"Lollie!" I laugh in spite of my misery.

She eases Milly Molly Mandy into the traffic and waves her hand vaguely at the stereo. "Music, darling, sort it. We must have music!"

"Amen to that."

Coming home to the cottage is blissful and sad all at once. Doris is waiting, and so is my beautiful oak. But knowing Johnny isn't here makes Fire Station Lane seem empty.

Clyde doesn't care. He is delighted to be home again and leaps about like a loon. Doris hugs me and invites Lollie inside, so I bump the wheels up the steps and go ahead of them both into the kitchen. "Tea, Doris? Coffee, Loll?"

"Perfect." Lollie is exploring the cottage. "You know, I've never seen inside this big bedroom, the door is usually closed."

"It was Alfred's library until I got tired of sleeping on the couch."

"Nice reno. Love the shawls." Lollie wheels down the hall. "What are you going to do now you're back?"

"I don't know. I still have my business to run, but it might be fun to have another project." I need to keep busy. Johnny has left a hole in my heart and my life.

Lollie is peeping into other rooms. "You've got a lot of records piled up in here."

"They're Alfred's," I explain. "We're not sure yet what to do with them."

Lollie circles the stacks, checks out a few of the covers. "These are great! All the classics. The Beatles, The Doors, Stevie Nicks, Tina Turner. You should open a record shop."

I stare at her. "We don't have a record shop in Mayton."

She nods sagely. "We don't have a record shop."

"Doris," I call, "what do you think about starting a record shop with Alfred's vinyl collection?"

Doris comes to the door of the kitchen. "Yes, if it will stop you playing those abominations at full volume."

"I thought you liked hearing them?"

"Not those awful, noisy songs from skinny, half-naked men with big hair and eye makeup."

"That's glam rock, Doris, it's awesome. T-Rex, David Bowie, Slade, Suzi Quatro, Queen, they're all legends." I look at Lollie. "Running a record shop would be actual fun."

"It would," she grins. "I'll come every day to annoy you and buy stuff."

"I could do it part-time, in-between my architecture projects – selling online and instore."

"Now you're talking."

I hug my friend. "Lollie, did I tell you I love you?"

"It's a given, girlfriend."

I pour coffee for myself and Lollie, and make tea for Doris. I give Doris a recipe book I found in Auckland, *101 Satisfying Ways with Toast*. She laughs and pats my hand in thanks.

She is not smiling when she wakes me at 1AM. She is screaming. I kick off my covers and race into her room. Clyde is ahead of me, and he whines at her bedside. "Doris, are you OK?"

Doris is wide-eyed, sweating and disoriented. I feel a prickle of fear. I want to run away, but instead I lean in to hug her, tidy her bedclothes, offer her a glass of water. Slowly, her eyes refocus.

"Alfred's granddaughter," she says, her gaze fixed on my face.

"Yes. I'm Quinn, remember?"

"That awful dog."

"Clyde."

She takes a sip of water. "I had a nightmare, I think."

"I haven't heard you do that before. Wake up screaming."

"I think I only started doing it... a few weeks ago. I don't like being here by myself. I forget, I..." She struggles to express herself, and tears well up. "I miss Alfred so much."

"Oh, Doris I'm sorry, I should have realised." I perch on the bed and take her hand. "You know, I think we should tell Hemi we're not selling the house. I will stay here with you. We'll make it work."

"I don't want you to be... inconvenienced."

I squeeze her hand. "I like being here. With you." *I do. Even without Johnny.* Doris kisses my fingers and I blink back tears. Who knew I could learn to love having a step-grandmother?

Her face lights up. "I would like that."

"I'll tell Hemi tomorrow." We hug, and snuggle together and chat about her photos until she is ready to go back to sleep.

Then I lie awake for ages, thinking about Doris. In the ignorance of youth, I've never thought properly about what these big changes – a sudden bereavement, and my arrival – meant for her. With her memory not what it was, this ever-changing world is a confusing and scary place for Doris.

Lollie said that she popped in a few times while I was away, and Shirley dropped round with groceries, but Doris has been alone for many hours. She can get around town using Bert's taxi and her walking cane, but being so frail now, she prefers someone to be with her.

I sigh. "Clyde, we haven't been the best step-grandchildren. In fact, we've been thoughtless and dumb."

Clyde thinks I should speak for myself. He's busy chasing rabbits in his dreams.

The next morning, I make tea for Doris and leave a message for Hemi about not selling the house. Then I take Clyde for a run. It's very early, there's a frost on the ground and little birds sitting hunched and fluffy on the power lines. I turn onto Main Street and almost crash into Johnny, coming out of his house. I can't believe it. He is staying at his mamma's house? Just across the road?

I fix him in place with a smile. "Buongiorno!"

He flinches and I almost feel sorry. "Good morning, Quinn."

"Nice to see your house in use again. Must be more comfortable than the Station. Will you be doing any work to it?" I have so many questions. The one I really want to ask – 'Where the hell have you been?' – is frozen on my tongue.

"I don't know." His voice is rough, his gaze shuttered. "It is Mamma's house and she won't talk about it. I don't know." He scrubs his hand through his hair.

I want to hug him and say I don't care what happened between us, your mama loves you but she's just going through a thing, come back to me I miss you. Instead I say cheerfully, "I got home yesterday from Auckland."

He looks awkward. "I know."

"It was way too crowded with three of us in my mother's apartment, so we flew back here." Johnny's jaw goes tight and he looks as though he could kill someone. I wonder if his scar is hurting him. "Clyde was driving me crazy. City life really doesn't suit him."

"Clyde the Collie?" Johnny sucks in air like a man drowning. Is that a smile? I wait for more, but that's it.

My despair boils into outrage. "Two weeks, Johnny, and not a word! Why?"

He looks at me helplessly. Glory, if he can't find the words I will never know. I'll spend another decade wondering what happened.

But then he surprises me. He touches me on the lips with one broad, brown thumb. "Bella, you are sunshine." What? That is very cool. He is saying that to me? "But you need to stay away from me. Please. You deserve better."

"Uh?" I'm still back at the 'Bella you are sunshine' bit.

"I'm not right for you. I don't know if I can keep you safe. I couldn't keep Mario safe! What if something happens and..."

"What are you talking about, Johnny? I don't need to be kept *safe*. I want to enjoy life – just be together, have some fun – you know, *breathe*!" With you. Please. "Is this something to do with your brother? Your house?" I stare at this beautiful, silent, infuriating man whom I am impossibly, infuriatingly in love with.

He looks at me. "I... have to go."

"Wait! Johnny, please."

His voice cracks. "I can't, Quinn."

He walks away. I look down at Clyde. "Was that an answer? I don't think that was an answer. How can I fix this if I don't know what the hell he's talking about?"

Johnny's mind is in turmoil. He doesn't understand why Quinn is back. And how can he just *be* with her? He wants so much from her, but he cannot put any of it into words and she deserves better.

It is impossible, bella. I will hurt you. I'll fail you. You are my bright, happy, beautiful Quinn, but you deserve someone better. Someone confident and capable, like that Spanish man.

Anyway, what happened to him? I thought he was in Auckland with you.

Going for my run doesn't help my mood. Clyde is so excited to be home, he drags me into every ditch and every garden and wraps me round every power pole. I get home feeling cross and completely over it, shut him inside and go down to complain to Lollie.

It is Saturday morning so Adam is sleeping in, but Lollie is in her garden. She makes coffee and we wander out to sit on her lawn. Mayton is just starting to wake up. We can see Olive opening up her serving window, and Lori and her boys driving past on their way to the pool for swimming lessons. The twins are wearing their goggles. We wave, and they wave, Taika nearly falling out of the car in his enthusiasm.

"Johnny is back at his mum's house?" Lollie's brows go up when I tell her. "Wow. That's some deep psychological stuff going on, right there."

"You mean about his brother and his car, and..."

"No, I mean Johnny. We're talking about Johnny, right? I don't know anything about his car."

"It's not his... Oh, forget it. I don't know, Loll, I don't know about any of it – what he's doing and why, what he wants, and what on earth *I'm* going to do."

"You are going to open a record shop."

"I am. But I can't look at the Fire Station every day and see its lights on my ceiling every night and not think about Johnny. He is just so annoying and frustrating and confusing and..."

"Hot. Brooding. Sexy. I totally agree."

"When we were both fifteen, I asked him to kiss me. He remembers that."

"So do you, obviously." She grins. "Quinn, my dear, I have your diagnosis and it is very bad. We're possibly talking lifelong incapacitation here."

"Tell me about it," I laugh. But I really just want to cry.

Lollie rolls up to Johnny that evening in Café Diva and spins, her fairy lights twinkling. "Hey ho, Johnny Best, nice of them to put on a Saturday show this week. How are you?"

Johnny gives his half-smile. "Alright."

"Dance with me?"

"Not tonight."

She leans in. "I'm married, you know, but it's not serious. There's room for one more."

Johnny laughs. "No way. Adam would chase me off with his staple gun."

"That is true. And it's rather a large staple gun, so our affair is doomed." Lollie brightens. "Never mind, what I actually wanted to say is that you need to go and see Quinn. She is sitting at home as miserable as sin and it's all your fault."

Johnny's heart lurches. "How do you know it's my fault?"

"The same way I know that the sky is blue and you eat muesli for breakfast, Johnny Best. Because I see things and hear things and I love you and I love Quinn and I want you both to be happy. Right now, neither of you are." She taps Johnny on the nose with a lacquered nail, winks, and goes spinning away onto the dance floor.

Johnny picks up his drink, puts it down again. He leans back in his chair, stretches out his legs, crossing them at the ankle. So, Lollie knows stuff. Quinn still wants him, despite his ineptitude.

Idly watching the band, he begins to wonder if he's got it all wrong. Hope creeps stealthily back.

Chapter 21

I've missed Friday night at Diva's, and the Saturday night show they put on for Dave's birthday. I am feeling depressed, irritable and boring. Doris and I watch two episodes of The Bill, then go early to bed. Clyde is already asleep, twitching and dreaming of power poles.

I wake to a shower of stones against my window. "Hssst, Quinn Walker!" Clyde leaps up barking, cocks his head to listen, then whines. "Hsst, wake up!"

I open the sash. "Lollie, why are you throwing stones? And no one says 'Hssst' anymore."

Lollie is parked on my lawn in the moonlight. "Hsst is more fun, don't you think? Just like in a storybook."

"Have you been drinking?"

There is a crash as Billie falls out of the vine above my porch. "No way. (hic) Just a liddle bit."

"Whoa, Billie, that dress is stunning." I can't believe I've come back to this.

"Like it?" Billie twirls and trips over the doormat. "(hic) 's vintage."

Lollie grins. "We've been at Diva's but the band packed up and we wanted to crack on. Adam's away so I walked home with Billie..." They giggle. "Well, I *rolled* home with Billie. No, actually that sounds way worse. Anyway, we've come to get you, let's go down to the river."

"Why the river?" I ask.

Lollie draws herself to full height in her chair. "Have you been to the river on a night like tonight?"

"What's so special about tonight?"

"Full (hic) moon," Billie explains, looking sage. "It's glro (hec) glorious."

Lollie claps her hands. "It's a night for witches and warlocks, cats walking under ladders and strange, strange occurrences that will chill your bones, Quinn. Come on, you gotta come."

I feel a slow smile and the tingle of adventure. "Give me a minute to get dressed."

"No (hic) time for that. Come in your pj's. By the way, you're driving."

Lollie nods. "Yep. We'll take Milly Molly Mandy, but you have to drive. My brother-in-law will kill me if he catches me drinking and driving – then my sister will kill him and Christmas will be a real depressing event for my parents, you know?"

"Alright, I'll drive." I throw my wool coat over my shortie pyjamas, drag on hiking boots and tuck my driver's licence into my pocket.

Billie giggles. "Cute teddy bear."

"This is no time for fashion comparisons, you two." Lollie leads the way down the lane. "My car keys are on a rack inside the back door, Quinn, the house is unlocked. We'll meet you at the car."

Milly Molly Mandy starts first try and I feel a moment of envy. She feels luxurious to drive after the ancient Morris. I turn left on Main Street and head for the river.

"Park here." Lollie points at the boat ramp.

"No (hec) way, that's slippery after rain. Park on the grass."

I am firm. "I'm going to park on the gravel. There is no traffic this time of night, and if I drive off the road Milly is bound to get stuck in the mud."

Billie looks at me admiringly. "You are so sensible."

"I've never been called sensible in my life, but since I met you two I'm beginning to think..."

Lollie interrupts, "Aw, look at the river shining in the moonlight."

"Just like (hic) that Jipperson... *Jefferson* Starship song..."

I frown. "No, that's Dancing in the Moonlight."

"Is not! (hic hec) That bloke Chris Lane sings Dancing..."

Lollie yelps, "Shhh! Is that a baby crying?"

The three of us freeze.

"Why would there (hic) be a baby out here?"

My skin is prickling. "Surely not. At least, I hope not..."

Lollie laughs. "It's not a baby, it's a cat! See? Up there in the tree." She rolls closer to the big old macrocarpa on our left, bumping over the grass. "Ohmigod it's *my* cat!"

"You have a cat?" I ask.

"It's my witch's familiar."

"Your what?"

Lollie cups her mouth with her hands. "Esmé, come down from there!"

Billie shines her phone torch upwards. "Ohmigod ohmigod (hic) look Lollie, she's stuck up the tree!"

Lollie shrieks. "Oh no, she's stuck! Quick, Quinn, do something."

"Why me?"

"You're the most sober woman here. And you *like* climbing trees."

Seriously. "*Cats* like climbing trees! She'll be fine, Loll, don't panic. If I climb all the way up there, she'll just jump down and make me look stupid. Then *I'll* have to climb all the way back down and..."

"I offer you the hand of friendship but when I really need you – worse, when my *cat* needs you – you turn your face aside."

"Lollie, you're being dramatic. Stop looking at me like that, both of you. Cats are good at climbing trees. It's what they do."

Billie objects, "Esmé is *stuck*, Quinn. Stuck! See (hic) her poor sad face up there. If you won't go up and save her (hec) I will."

I meet her jutting gaze. "Please don't, you know what happened last time you..."

"Dishperat- (hic) desperative times and all." Billie slithers into the bole of the huge macrocarpa, hitches her dress awkwardly against the rough bark and begins to climb.

I groan. "That's vintage Dior silk you're ruining." Another thought occurs and I groan again, "If Johnny gets another call out, Thea is going to kill me. I'll be arrested for wasting emergency resources on cats and Billie." I cup my hands and yell, "If you're going to risk your neck, at least take your high heels off!"

Billie's voice floats back. "A girl's gotta do (hic) what a girl's gotta do. If I have to die in a red pair of heels, then..."

"Nobody's going to die!" I bellow.

Lollie looks thoughtful. "You know, she might." When I glare at her, she says, "It's Billie. *Inebriated*. In a tree."

"Alright, alright, you've made your point. And she'll definitely ruin that dress. I'm going up."

It is inevitable that the inevitable happens. Billie gets to the cat before me, and grabs it. There is an almighty feline screech, a Billie screech, a frantic scrabble and they both fall.

"Ohmigod ohmigod..." she shrieks. "Oh, good catch, Quinn! And I'm not (hic) upside down this time."

"I've got you, hold on tight, don't look down." Wedged in a fork of the macrocarpa, breathing fast, I have Billie gripped with my right hand and the cat in my left. Billie is giving me the most trouble. "Hold onto my waist and don't move, whatever you do. If you fall from here you'll land on the rocks."

Billie clutches me. "All good, we're sweet now."

I am panting with exertion and pain. "Not really, but we're alive, which is a bonus. Just hang on while I get this..." a protesting screech, "claw out of my eye socket."

When I have Billie more or less secured and the cat stowed under my arm, four sets of claws variously sunk into my ribs and the side of my face, I become aware of a screeching below.

"Billie, Billie, Quinn, tell me, is that Esmé? Ohmigod ohmigod did she fall?"

"We're OK, Lollie!" I reassure her.

"But how's Esmé?"

I pause. "Who?"

Billie hiccups, "(hec) She's talking about the cat."

"Oh. Esmé's fine. Billie and I are too, in case you're wondering."

"Ooh, how wonderful, it's like that book, Cat Up a Tree! Do you think there are any more cats up there?" Lollie wheels over the bumpy grass, tipping back to look high into the tree. "Is Esmé coping? Give her a cuddle, Quinn, she's sensitive, she'll need reassurance."

"Not as sensitive as the skin on my arm, I think it's shredded."

"What did you say?" The chrome on her chair winks in the moonlight.

"Never mind."

"How are you going up there, Esmé? My diddikins, my fluffy wuffy peachy poo, my loveliest... Oops." There is a scuffle, a couple of heavy thumps and a splash.

"That doesn't sound good." I crane my neck to look down. "Loll, are you alright?"

There is a worryingly long pause, then she says, "Um. No worries. My wheels went into the river but I'm all good."

"*What?*" I yelp.

"Bloody (hic) hell, Lollie!"

"It's fine. I never liked them anyway."

I can't believe how calm she sounds. "You mean they've gone into the *water?*"

"Yes, but not with me. I fell out. Like I said, I didn't like them anyw..."

Billie coughs. "I don't want to be insensiti... insensible, Loll (hec) but don't you need them?"

Lollie laughs, wriggling into a sitting position on the damp, rough grass. "Don't worry, my good chair is at home. Adam can go fishing for my wheels later. Or they'll be like Scuffy the Tugboat and go floating down to the sea."

Billie murmurs across our precarious perch, "Do you (hic) know what Loll is talking about?"

"Yes, everyone knows Scuffy. He floated downriver to the ocean, got caught on a fishing line and ended up in a bath."

"Weird. Although (hic) I'd like a hot bath right now."

"Don't think about it, it'll just make you feel colder." I try to move, then stop as Billie slips downwards. Ignoring her squeals and the digging claws of the cat, I study by moonlight the tangle of human limbs, tree limbs and furry cat limbs wrapped around me. I hate to admit it, but I don't think I can get Billie out of here by myself. Let alone the familiar.

I sigh. "I think we need help, Billie. But we can't ring Johnny. Do you know anyone else with a really, really long ladder?"

"Totally not. Johnny has the longest (hec) ladder in town. Hey Loll, ring Johnny!"

"Johnny who?" Lollie must be very drunk.

"Johnny Best. You know (hic) hot firefighter, great abs, buns of..."

"Oh yeah."

"...steel."

"*Ay*, you two, you need to stop objectifying firefighters."

Billie taps my nose. "You can't talk (hic) you're the one who's been walking round in his shirt."

"Don't mention that. I can't believe you mentioned that. Is there no privacy in this miniscule town?"

"Nope (hec). Mayton. No privacy. You should've heard (hic) fuss when I went off with a movie mogul."

Lollie's voice floats up. "He was a movie mogul? I heard he was a porn star producer."

Billie gives a scandalised yelp. Then after a brief pause, "You know (hic) that would've been more interesting."

Lollie is fiddling with her phone. "Hey, Johnny, is that you?"

Now I yelp. "I told you we can't ring Johnny!"

"(hic) Shush, Quinn. Johnny is totally the guy we need in a situation like this. Buns of steel can only help in a crisis. You know, like Rocky."

I glare at Billie. "It's Superman."

"What?"

"Superman is the Man of Steel, not Rocky."

"Whatever (hic). S'long as he brings his really long ladder."

I groan. "But I don't want him to come."

Billie looks astonished. "Why? You know (hec) it's Johnny Best, right? *I'd* want him to come. Lollie wants him to come. I bet half the women of Mayton want him to..."

"Because we broke up, that's why!"

Billie blinks. "You know he's ripped, right? (hic) Buns of steel. Why in the world would you break up with..."

"Johnny? Hey, Johnny, it's me. Who? Oh, Lollie. Lollie Barrington. You know, big hair, shiny wheels, I live next door to... Yeah, sorry to call this late but can you bring your ladder? We're down at the river. The river. We have a tree situation here. Billie is up a tree and... Yep, Quinn's here too, but that's not the prob-, hang on, how did you know?" A pause. "What do you mean, 'No, too much paperwork?' What has Quinn got to do with paperwork? See, my familiar was stuck in a tree so Billie went up the tree to get her, then Quinn went up to help *her* and... Oh, you know the story already." Lollie holds the phone out from her ear. "Quinn, I don't speak Italian but this sounds like expletives to me, it's kind of a universal thing."

I groan.

"But (hic) is he coming or what?" Billie is getting impatient.

"Are you coming?" Lollie asks the phone. "Nah, he's hung up already. Do you think I should ring him back?"

"Definitely not." I am emphatic.

"Yes (hic), we need his buns of steel and his huge... (hic) ladder."

I snap, "Billie, I am so going to wring your neck."

She looks smug. "You can't. You have to hold onto Esmé. If you drop Esmé (hic) you'll break Lollie's heart."

Lollie yelps. "Ohmigod ohmigod Quinn, don't drop Esmé!"

"Shut up, both of you, I am not going to drop Esmé!"

A brief pause. "(hic) There's no need to shout."

I thunk my head against the tree and immediately regret it. The bark of the macrocarpa is gnarled and thickly ridged, and Esmé protests by digging her claws deeper into my arm. I shift a little, trying to make us both more comfortable, but Esmé hisses. "Lollie, why do you have such a psychotic cat?"

"Isn't she cool?" Lollie says proudly. "She was the fiercest kitten in the litter. She fought with everyone, even her siblings. She bit Adam when we went to meet her, she's a total doll. So cool."

I look dubiously at Esmé. "She bit Adam, and you still thought it was a good idea to bring her home?"

"Of course."

"Adam agreed to that?"

"Adam always says yes."

Billie nodded. "(hic) It's true. Adam always says yes."

"Billie!" Lollie squawks.

"I mean to *you*, Lollie. He always says (hec) yes to you." Billie claps a hand over her mouth and nearly falls out of the tree. "Ohmigod did you think I meant...?"

"Well, what am I supposed to think when *you* of all people say..."

"Excuse you. (hic) How rude!"

"Everybody calm down!" I snap. "Billie, zip it. Loll, no one is casting aspersions at your husband. Are they?" I glare at Billie in the pale wash of moonlight.

"No (hic) 'spersions."

"Alright then." Lollie settles more comfortably in the grass. "It's really nice here. We should come down to the river more often."

"Maybe in daylight," I mutter.

"We could bring a picnic. I have the best picnic basket ever. It suits Milly Molly Mandy perfectly. Woven wickerwork, cute spotted napkins, little pockets for the wine bottles and the buns..."

Billie straightens up. "Speaking of buns (hic) is that the fire truck?"

"Ooh, Quinn, he's coming to your rescue!"

"Just like (hec) Rocky."

I groan. "Superman!"

"(hic) What?"

"Forget it."

Johnny arrives in a swirl of silent flashing lights and emotions. His feelings are indescribable as he jumps down from the truck and strides to the tree. Worry. A rush of connection. Fear. This close, he can feel her, even though she is clinging umpteen feet up a macrocarpa tree and is in trouble again. As Grant runs round to prep the ladder, Johnny goes first to check on Lollie, sitting on the ground.

She is calm. "My wheels went into the river but it's OK, it was my old chair."

"*Oddio*," Johnny exclaims, "into the river?"

"I'm fine, honest. It's Quinn we need to worry about. She is holding onto Billie and my cat, and if she drops my cat it will be the end of my world, I tell you. Adam's too."

"Nice!" squeaks a voice from the tree.

"It's true, Billie. Esmé is my chosen one, my familiar, my sister from another mother..."

"Gawd (hic)."

"My precious best friend, my feline guide to the spiritual realms..."

"Spare me," says a third voice.

Bella. Johnny cups his mouth and calls, "Quinn!"

"I'm here," she sighs.

"Good evening."

"Not from where I'm sitting."

"How imminently will you fall and die?"

"Not immediately." She sounds resigned. "Say, fifteen minutes before my patience runs out and I throttle Billie and jettison the cat."

Billie squawks. "(hec) Fifteen minutes? That's not long enough, I don't wanna die! I was gonna marry Brad and walk the Great Wall of China, start a hot yoga studio in the back of my shop..."

Lollie perks up. "Hot yoga? Cool, I'll come along to that..."

"Shut up, both of you!" Quinn yells.

Johnny cuts in. "Alright, I can be up the ladder in five. Hang in there."

"Ha (hic) hah de ha."

Johnny is as good as his word. He gets an unexpected eyeful of Quinn in her shortie pyjamas and nearly falls out of the tree, but manages to hold it together. He untangles all the legs and arms wrapped around her, tucks the feisty little cat into his shirt and gets them all down with a Billie-minimum of fuss.

"Esmé, you're safe at last, diddikins, my fluffy wuffy coochie coo!"

"I'm fine, Loll (hec) thanks for asking."

While Grant doles out blankets for everyone, Johnny looks hard at Quinn in the lights of the truck. "Are you hurt?" Her face is pale but she shakes her head, avoiding his gaze. "And Billie, how are you?"

"My dress will never be the same but I'm (hic) good, ta."

He turns to Lollie. "I'm going to assume the cat's fine."

"I don't know if you can assume that, Johnny Best. My Esmé is a very sensitive soul."

Johnny grins. "Tell that to the Vet tomorrow. I rescue cats, I don't treat them. Now, ladies, can I take you home in the engine or do you want to drive yourselves?" He pauses. "*Should* any of you drive?"

"(hic) Not me, and definitely not Lollie. She lost her wheels in the river. But Quinn is sober as a post."

He looks at her. "Really? And you still got tangled up with this lot?" She shrugs, and Johnny scrubs his face tiredly. "Will you be right to drive Milly Molly Mandy home?"

Her eyes glitter. "Yes."

"Grazie. Now let's get you all home. Lollie, may I?" He scoops Lollie off the grass and lifts her into the truck.

"Biceps of steel, too," Billie coos. Johnny steps aside for her to climb in beside Lollie. Grant closes the lockers and jumps up onto the side of the engine.

Johnny pauses, turns back to Quinn. "I told you to stay out of trees with Billie."

Her chin goes up. "What could I do, let her fall?"

He sighs. *You are so small and determined. Impulsive. Fierce.* "No. You couldn't let her fall." *You are amazing.* He wants to wrap this beautiful, bedraggled woman in his arms and apologise for everything dumb he's ever done and all the things he's failed to tell her. The important things, like *I love you.* He wants to kiss her and promise to rescue her anytime she needs it, forever amen, even with a million crazy friends and their cats.

But Grant and the others are waiting. He swings up into the truck.

Johnny asks if I am alright. I want to tell him no, I am scratched and grazed all over, I am sore, tired and missing you. I climb into Lollie's little striped car feeling overwhelmingly sad. Maybe this is the problem. Johnny thinks I'm irresponsible. He needs someone safe and sensible, someone who won't make him worry.

I know that he disapproves of me and this whole thing is impossible. I am cold, exhausted, and still in shock that I actually managed to catch Billie and the cat. That was a Guinness Book of World Records' catch. I'd thought we were all going to die.

Johnny eases his truck up the bank onto the gravel track. I follow him back to Mayton, barely able to see the road for my tears.

Chapter 22

In the morning, I clip on Clyde's lead and start down the lane. Johnny is standing motionless in the street by his bike, deep in thought. To me, he looks like he's surrounded by ghosts – the great red car lying covered in dust in the garage, the house behind him in its tangle of ivy, filled with the clutter of a family long disintegrated.

I nod as I jog past.

"Quinn."

It is still a caress, the way he says it. Will I ever get over that?

I stop, and Clyde wraps me up in the lead. "Hang on." I untangle myself. Is that a glint of amusement in his eyes? Midnight. Save me. "What?" I want to sound like I have a million better things to do this morning than stand here in the street looking at Johnny.

"I'm sorry." His voice is husky. Divine.

"What for?" Just come over here and kiss me, already. You make me feel incredible and I miss that so, so...

"For growling. Last night. I realise you are not responsible for Billie."

"Yes, that'd be a nightmare." It's definitely a glint. I blunder on. "Can I see you today? Just to talk, you know, I..."

"I can't. There's something I need to do."

"What is so important?" Don't overdo it, Quinn.

"Paperwork." His smile quirks.

"Can I help?" I am overdoing it.

"No." He shrugs on his jacket and starts his bike. I watch him ride away. He is not going to do paperwork from the saddle of his Harley. I decide that it will take me at least three decades of running, more if Clyde comes with me, to work off all my frustration, confusion, lust and attraction for this beautiful, infuriating man.

"Ciao, Mamma." He walks into her room and reaches for her hand. She stiffens but does not look at him. He kneels by her chair and looks into her face, at those fine, dark eyes that will not meet his. He speaks in Italian so there is no chance she can misunderstand.

"Mamma, I am going to clean up the house. The garden is overgrown, the inside is covered in dust and all our things are getting old. They have no purpose now – the furniture, the linen and bedclothes, sports gear, Mario's things..." Johnny's voice breaks, and her hand convulses in his. "I am sorry, but I have to do it. It has been a long time. Rosa says you don't want to live there ever again, so I will clean the house, give away the things we don't want, and find a nice family to live there. Let it be a home again." He watches her face for a long, silent moment, then gently untangles his fingers from hers. "Alright now, Mamma, I will go."

He is almost at the door when she speaks. Her voice is barely a whisper but it is like a miracle to him. "Johnny. Bring...

Mario's rosary beads to me. His sports medals. Your father's hat."

"Of course."

"And the photographs."

"Sì, Mamma. All the photographs." He pauses. "Do you want Mario's car?"

She flicks her hand. "I hate that noisy red car."

"Then I will have it."

A smile flickers across Mamma's face. Her eyes are suddenly, startlingly full of love and humour. "I hope you drive better than Mario."

Johnny's smile flashes. "Always."

I am pathetic. I am listening for his bike, so I know exactly when he gets home. The clock above the TV ticks by six awful minutes of waiting, then there's a thundering knock at the door. Doris hears it over her program and looks up, startled.

I hug her. "Don't worry, it's Johnny." It's Johnny! I beat Clyde to the door. Then I freeze, because what if he's not here to see me, what if he's just dropping in groceries for Doris, or...

Johnny puts his palm to the glass. "Let me in?" The lights of the Station dance behind him. I press my palm against his on the glass, small in the silhouette of his large one, and wonder what keeps me here in this complicated dance with this complicated man.

He clears his throat. "I wanted to say this earlier, Quinn, but there's something I had to, um... I know things aren't right."

If he is here to tell me off again about last night... "What are you talking about?"

"Quinn, please, I want to tell you..."

"Just say it already."

"I'm trying to." He rubs his hand through his hair. "*Mamma mia*, Quinn. Without you, all the brightness is gone."

Glory. I open the door and Clyde throws himself at Johnny's legs. I leap into Johnny's arms and he reels with the double impact. "Clyde, down boy." He holds me tight. "Ciao, bella. Are you OK?"

I am laughing through my tears. "No, I'm not. You've ruined me for anything, and anyone else. I can't think, I can't design a house to save myself, I cry all the time..."

"I am sorry."

I scrub at my tears. "Why did you leave?"

"I saw you with that bloke. In the park."

"You saw me with José?" The pennies fall into place. "You thought I'd get back together with José? Why didn't you ask me?" He looks sheepish and I glare at him. "Bloody hell, Johnny, you need to think less and talk more."

He grins, the wide one, the smile that kills me. "I know."

I realise I should be fair. "And I should probably think more and talk less."

"*No*, bella, you are just right."

I try to explain. "José doesn't mean anything to me, honestly, he's a complete tosser. His father needs me for their Olympic contract, to design the next Village, so he came here to beg me to move back and work for them. Az brought him to Mayton and that was such a low thing for her to do, I don't know if I can ever..."

Johnny pulls me into a hug. His body wraps around me, hard and strong. I stop talking and just breathe him in. I want to stay like this forever. I want to run my fingers over his beautiful, scarred face and kiss him until... I step back. "Come in?" Now. Please!

He shakes his head. "I'm on duty tonight. I just wanted to..." He searches for the words. "Come here. See you. Make it right."

"Oh. OK."

"Right."

"Well then." What is it about Johnny that I can just look at him for hours? I resist the urge to grab a fistful of his official-looking shirt and drag him into my bed. It is difficult. Maybe if I just leap on him, right here in the...

"'Notte, bella." Johnny steps off the porch.

I frown. "Clyde, I've made a tactical error. Lady Hatwick would not have worried about creasing his uniform. She would've just grabbed him."

Johnny goes home with his head and his heart full of Quinn. At first he'd wondered if Quinn just wanted him for sex, but she seems to genuinely want him in her life. She said she was ruined for anyone else. It's a nice thing to say, but he hardly believes it.

He forces back his doubts. They have got him into trouble before. Life without Quinn is less than. He will ignore his inner caution. He wants more.

But first, there is work to do.

Chapter 23

That night there is a fire in the industrial area east of Mayton. I hear the fire engine roll out about midnight, its lights on in the darkness but no siren because of the late hour. Flashing lights wheel briefly across my ceiling.

I hear from Lollie in the morning that the fire burned down three sheds and a data centre, but no one was hurt. It does, however, result in three days of mopping up by the fire crews and more paperwork for Johnny and Thea. I barely see anyone from the Fire Station all week, but the truck comes and goes and I see Johnny crossing the road back to his house at the end of his shift.

I am not stalking him, truly. He doesn't come to see me but I figure he's distracted. I am trying out a new, calmer, less frenetic me.

This new me has a lot of work to do that I've neglected in recent weeks. I make tea and buttery French toast for Doris, and together we turn her vegetable garden over and mulch it, ready for winter. I finish renovation plans for two clients and get three new concept plans started.

By Wednesday evening, we've settled into a routine that is way too domesticated and I am desperate. I choose 'London Calling' with its guitar-smashing cover, put it on and dance around the room. With Doris waving her stick at The Clash, or perhaps at me, and Clyde jumping, I lose myself in the crackle and hiss of warped vinyl on Alfred's ancient record player.

The mechanical crackle that wakes me the next morning is far louder, throatier and sexier. My heart leaps. I scramble out of bed to look down the lane.

"Is it thunder?" Doris pokes her head out her door.

"No, come and look!" I am laughing and waving with joy. Hope. Delight.

A red '72 De Tomaso Pantera is edging its snout round the corner, easing over the kerb. Its engine is snarling, rattling windows all the way up the lane. "Clyde don't worry, it is not going to eat you!"

There is no doubt, I have seen that car before. This time it is cleaner, sleeker and even more red. With all the dust gone, a fat black racing stripe is visible, streaking up the bonnet and over the roof. The driver is tall, dark-haired and unmistakably Italian.

I struggle to pull on my bra, get the straps in a knot and toss it in a corner. I drag on indigo jeans, pull a pinot red poncho over my head and run out the door. I run back in for my purse and my shoes. I kiss Doris on the cheek, and run back out with Clyde.

Skipping down the steps, I meet the Pantera by my picket gate. This close, the engine is impossibly loud. The whole car vibrates with the throb of its pistons.

"Uh uh." Johnny shakes his head. "No way. *No.*"

"But Clyde wants to come."

"Mario says no dogs."

There is no arguing with Mario. I hustle Clyde back to the cottage and shut him in. I slide into the passenger seat. The V8 coupe rocks beneath us. The interior smells of polish and Johnny's aftershave. I purr, "Do you know how sexy this car is?"

"Sì."

"Does Mario mind me coming?"

The flash of a grin. "Mario never said no to a woman in his life."

"What are we doing?"

Johnny eases the coupe onto Main Street, heading for the Remutaka Hills. "We are breathing."

Mario's car is an exhilarating ride through the hills, its great engine crackling into corners and snarling out the other side. Johnny drives like he always does, thoughtful, intense, gives a trademark quirk of his mouth whenever the car does something fun, perfect, fast. Quinn rolls down her window and laughs into the wind.

At the highest point of the range, they pull into the parking bay to watch the rising sun climb the sky. The shadows are long, the air crisp and brittle with light.

Quinn launches from the car like a cannonball, throwing herself across the gleaming bonnet. "This car, Johnny, it's wonderful! J'adore! Oops, sorry, that's French." She dances across the carpark and onto the barrier guards. "I am glad you brought it out to play."

Johnny smiles as she pirouettes on the barrier rail, lifting her face to the light. "Look at those baby rimu trees, Johnny, they're so happy in the gully, sheltered from the wind. And see the flax leaves shining. I love it here, so cold but so beautiful."

Johnny leans against the car, taking in the view, letting Quinn's energy and chatter wash over him. He has been working hard clearing out his childhood home, sorting through Mario's things, taking all the important stuff to Mamma. It has been emotional, exhausting, cathartic. And while he worked on Mario's car he felt the pieces come together at last – he knows now that he's done all he could, that Mamma will forgive him, that he has spent enough time with his life on hold and his heart a frozen wasteland.

Quinn was right about his brother. About the house. About this car. Quinn's impulsive, intuitive heart is right about a lot of things, he considers, but it will all be for nothing if she falls off that barrier and down four hundred metres of scree.

He steps into her line of sight. "Quinn! Let's drive to a vineyard for lunch."

"Great idea! Oops, hang on, yep, all good." She extracts herself haphazardly from the safety barrier and jumps into his arms.

Johnny wraps himself round this tumble of merino and denim, all legs, blonde ponytail and bright eyes. "Ready, sunshine?"

"Ready."

He bundles her into the passenger seat. "Any particular vineyard?"

"Any. Take me away, Johnny!"

They drive out of the hills in silence. Quinn is admiring the view and Johnny is lost in his thoughts. Driving this car brings Mario closer. He can hear his voice again, his laugh, all

Johnny's memories of his brother supercharged by the growl of the Pantera.

He turns into a road lined with vineyards. "I want to tell you what happened to Mario." He is pleased that his voice is not shaking. Quinn's gaze cuts to him and he tries to get his thoughts straight. "The night Mario died, he stayed late at work." He clears his throat, pauses to shift up. "Mamma wanted him to be a lawyer but he loved being with cars. All he wanted to do when we got back from Europe was learn to be a mechanic."

He shifts down into the corner, accelerates onto the straight. "He stayed back to weld a friend's car. Something to do with the chassis. He asked me to help but I was on duty. When the call came through, I was at a road accident. Thea and Grant took the small unit but they really needed the truck. By the time I got there the fire was fully involved, there were gas bottles on site, fuel stores, not a hope of stopping it."

Quinn watches the open country roll by, light and dark flashing in stripes as they drive past hedged windbreaks. Johnny puts his hand absently to his face. "I went in to find Mario. Thea said no, but I went in anyway. The fire was roaring, there was so much smoke..." His voice broke. "It was bad. Mario was unconscious so I had to carry him, but before I got out the oxy cylinders exploded. I woke up in hospital. My brother didn't make it."

Her voice is quiet. "Johnny, stop the car."

He looks at her face and pulls over onto the shoulder. Quinn climbs past the gear shift into his lap. He says into her hair, "I should have been there."

"You were out on a job. How could you know what would happen?"

"Mario was a terrible welder, he never paid attention to safety. I knew that."

"At some point Mario needed to take responsibility for himself."

Johnny is silent. He runs his fingers through her hair and she nestles closer. "I know. It's just taken me a while to work that out."

Quinn tips her face up. He leans in to kiss her, her lips soft against his. Their eyes meet, and hesitantly she reaches to touch his scar. She has this thing about it, but he doesn't mind. He leans into her hand. "It is OK, bella."

Her eyes sparkle and he kisses her again, feeling passion, grief, joy.

The Pantera idles gutturally.

He stirs. "Can we go? If we sit here too long, the car will overheat." *Or I will.* "Then we'll never get to the vineyard."

We stay out all day, cruising the vineyards and the hills. It is dark when Johnny parks the Pantera outside his family home and we walk across to Fire Station Lane.

"What a beautiful day." I put my hand in Johnny's and he kisses it. Alfred's cottage is ahead, framed by wisteria and the magnificent oak. Fuschia leaves glow silver in the light from the Station, and I wave my hand at them. "You know, it is never really dark here in the lane. Or quiet. But I don't mind."

Johnny pulls me close. "I used to hate the dark. I couldn't sleep. I'd walk most of the night instead."

"Why?"

"I don't know, Mario died in the night, the fire started at night, who knows, I just couldn't." His smile quirks. "It got better after you moved in."

"Really?"

"I liked seeing your lights. It meant you were here, too."

I pause on the porch steps. "*I* made you feel better?"

"Like I said, you are sunshine. For a while I still walked around, but really I just wanted to be here."

Glory. What a thing. I don't know whether to panic at the enormous responsibility right here, or jump into his arms and promise never to leave. "Johnny Best, step this way. Oops, watch out for Clyde. Doris will be asleep so we won't be interrupted and I want to make you coffee." Mm, and a whole lot else.

We make it as far as the kitchen, Clyde dancing around us. I put the kettle on, then give up any pretence at civilities and climb right into Johnny's lap. He hugs me tight, and I leaned into his warmth and strength. Clyde pushes his nose in, so I fondle his ears.

The clock above the servery cupboard ticks loudly. The fire pops and sparks, as hot coals break and scatter. Johnny looks at me. I know what he needs. If he doesn't, I certainly do. I shrug the shoulder of my poncho down, and his eyes follow. I run my hand along his jaw, slide my thumb in his mouth. He explores my thumbprint with his tongue, sucking it gently, his gaze fixed on my face. I can feel every nerve end tingling with that slow, wet, intimate caress. He kisses me, his mouth travelling down the line of my throat to my collarbone, my shoulder, down the curve of my...

He stops. "Are we going to do this in front of the dog?"

"Do what?" I am grinning.

"Keep looking like that, and I won't be responsible for my actions."

"Looking like what?"

Johnny punctuates each word with a butterfly kiss, "Beautiful. Sexy. Fun. Wicked. *Bellissima...* did I say sexy?"

"Ooh right, doggo, out!" I run Clyde out into the hall and shut the door. I push a chair against it so we'll have warning if Doris comes in. No need to give her a heart attack.

A dark wing lifts. "Where was I?"

"I think you got to the word 'sexy'." I slide back into his lap.

"Mmm." Johnny helps Quinn out of her poncho and jeans, his heart pounding, his blood running hot. He is desperate to touch all of her, have all of her, take her right here in the kitchen. It has been so long and he's been so lost, he can't believe he's found his way back to her. Perhaps Quinn has the same idea because she is enthusiastic, hauling his shirt up over his head and dragging at his belt buckle. Here's that teddy bear again, with no bra under. *Bella.* She moans as he caresses her breasts, kisses them, runs his hands down to cup her buttocks.

He pulls her close. She is rocking against him, right where she's freed his jeans and found hard, throbbing muscle. He pushes up her tee, hot blood coursing under his skin.

"Wait," she gasps. "Wait." Quinn wriggles out of her knickers. He slips on protection and her eyes are smiling as she locks her mouth on his. He is so afraid he'll hurt her, he moves slowly at first, but she wraps her thighs about him and urges him faster. Her fingers are tangled in his hair and her tongue down his throat, she clutches at him so he thrusts deeper, driving into her until he loses himself and she throws back her head joyfully, exultantly.

When they've both come back to earth, Johnny gazes at her face. *Bellissa, this beautiful woman.* She is wide-eyed with pleasure, her hair in her mouth, her scent on his skin, and he drinks in the sight of her. "See?" He is breathing hard. "Sexy."

"You've worked up a sweat in my kitchen," she purrs. "That's sexy, too."

When Clyde is allowed back in, he stands determinedly by the pantry door, tail wagging. "*Ay*, I forgot to feed him!" Quinn jumps up to give biscuits to the eager collie. "I'm hungry too. How about dinner? We have vegetarian korma to reheat, and basmati rice. I'll get it ready while you bring in some firewood."

He catches her hand as she walks past and kisses it. "Sì, bella."

Johnny works quietly around Quinn. He is content to be with her, see her, listen to her, kiss her. Anything else is wonderful. He loves her smile, her laughter, her energy, and he is happy to be here in her kitchen soaking her up.

Later, they make slow, gentle love in Quinn's bedroom. He revels in kissing her, in her taste, her answering touch on his skin. Together they explore and lose themselves in each other. The lights of the Fire Station are reflected in Quinn's eyes as she rears naked astride him. He is gentle with her, teasing. When she can bear it no longer, she bites down on his shoulder and he drives them to exquisite climax.

Quinn scoops up his hand and kisses it. "Bliss. I can't imagine what I've been doing with my evenings 'til now."

Johnny grins. "Hopefully not this." He is playing with her hair, catching the soft, shimmering strands in his fingers.

"No chance. Since our first kiss I've been ruined for anyone else."

"Me too." His smile is teasing. "But I knew you'd be trouble."

"Me? Trouble?"

He counts on his fingers. "I've been fixing fences, moving firewood, getting you out of trees, getting *Billie* out of trees, bringing your dog home every day, lying awake worrying you'll go back to Barcelona... See? Trouble."

"Well, now you can stay up all night for a different reason."

Johnny laughs, just as the thin wail of the Station siren slides like a knife into the night and begins to work itself up to full roar. He caresses her beloved face, shoulder, breast, rests his hand on the velvet curve of her hip. "I'd love to." He kisses her nose. "But I have to go to work."

She follows him to the door. He pulls on his jeans, drags his jersey over his head, pauses with one hand on the doorknob. "Can I see you again?" He barely dares to ask. "I mean... Not just in the lane."

"You really have to ask, after today? Yes, Johnny Best, come back or there *will* be trouble."

Chapter 24

I turn to see Doris standing in the hall, dishevelled with sleep. "Was that your man, Johnny whatsit?"

I feel like I'm fifteen and have been caught out by my mother. "Johnny Best. Yes."

"A silly name for an Italian."

"His father was English."

"Oh, that's alright then."

I feel we're drifting from the point. "Do you mind Johnny coming over?"

"Of course not, it's about time. He's yummy, I like him much better than that dratted dog." She gives her sudden, beaming smile. "Hurry up and ask Johnny to move in. I want the hall painted."

"You don't waste time, do you? Isn't your generation supposed to be prudish?" But I am still grinning as I climb back into bed. Johnny is so funny. He seems to have more confidence with his jeans off than on. In bed, he sets me on fire. He is kind, generous, sexy, teasing and demanding. With his clothes back on and the big, complicated world before him, he doubts his power to hold me.

"Jeeze," I tell Clyde, "He could do half as much and have me forever."

Clyde makes no comment. He wrestles his blankets into a pile and flops on top with a contented sigh. I lie watching the lights on my ceiling. Am I really thinking forever? I've never been this serious about a man. A year or two maybe, a specific trip or adventure, but not forever.

But then I've never felt like this. And that car... What a day! I loved every moment with that beautiful man and that beautiful car, racing through the hills, growling, pulsing, breathing, then coming home to... *Mamma mia*. Forever feels right when I'm with Johnny.

On Friday, I shake out my champagne satin dress and head to Diva's. The moon sheds flags of silver in the clouds and I am waiting, listening for Johnny. He rode down to Wellington today and is not back yet.

I am early so the band is still setting up. Mel and Sue are sitting at the bar watching them. Ira tells me my satin dress is the best thing to happen to Mayton since the Queen drove through town in her Daimler, in the summer of 1954. He puts me to work helping with his kit.

I am learning how to tighten the snare drum when Lollie arrives, with Kate and Linc and his guitars in tow. I join them at Sue's table. Billie arrives too, with Brad, and starts taking drink orders for the bar. Mel is fine, Sue asks for another gin and tonic and Lollie and I opt for the same. Brad orders a Coke.

Billie checks. "Just Coke? That's non-alcoholic, right?" Brad nods and she grins, then sashays to the bar. As Brad wanders off to greet his cousin, Linc raises an eyebrow at Sue.

She explains, "Billie says that if Brad turns over a new leaf, she'll marry him."

"He'll have to turn over a whole tree."

Sue tips the dregs of her drink over his head. "Don't be judgemental, I think it's sweet." Linc bails for the stage, shaking gin from his hair, and Sue looks ruefully at Kate. "Sorry. I forgot myself. Brothers can be so annoying."

Kate is laughing. "I hope Brad and Billie are very happy together. It will be great for both of them."

Lollie says, "What Billie wants, she gets. So, we know they'll be fine. Brad won't be *allowed* to put a foot wrong." She spins and her wheels light up. "Come on, you lot, let's dance!"

Linc starts in on *Seven Nation Army*, his bass vibrating through the floor, and Rae steps up to the mike. But I am listening for Johnny's Harley and soon I hear it over the music. I slip outside. Johnny is in his ubiquitous jeans and leather jacket, rolling his bike onto its stand.

He cuts his eyes to mine and I flush. "Hello, stranger."

"Quinn." He kisses me long and slow and I get squiggles in every unmentionable. I am about to suggest we go somewhere more private, but he opens the café door so I slide in under his arm. Warm light and music washes over us.

"Upon my soul, Johnny Best!" Lollie's bellow cuts through the intro bars of *Wagon Wheel* and every head turns. "You look *sizzling* hot tonight."

"Hands off, Lollie, you can't have him." I'm tucked against Johnny, his arm around my waist and his lips in my hair.

"Ssh, Lollie, they're playin' my song!"

"Shuddup, Morrie, I've got to inspect lover boy and my girlfriend here." Lollie spins around us, her fairy lights flashing. "You two make my heart sing. Wanna dance?"

"I was *born* for dancing," I tell her. Johnny releases me, and I pull Lollie onto the dance floor. Billie, Christa and Nessa Trelaney are already there in a gyrating, noisy crush. We call out to Johnny together and he soon gives in, shedding his jacket to join us with a self-effacing grin. He is accomplished at dancing with Lollie's wheels and he spins her deftly round. He weaves us all together in a free-flowing, comic dance improv until Lollie and the others are shrieking and I am breathless with laughter.

After a couple of numbers, he bows out and heads for the bar. I see Thea give him a triumphant look from across the room. *I knew she was The One for you.* Johnny ducks his head to hide a smile. We both know Thea will be insufferable after this.

"Same as usual?"

"Thanks, Trelaney." Johnny settles on a bar stool beside Kate.

She clinks her glass against his. "Cheers, you."

"Kate," he nods. "All good?" On stage, the band launches into a Creedence number. Ira tries a tricky stick twirl and his drumstick flies into the crowd. Catcalls ensue, but everyone dives to find the stick, Ira tapping the cowbell with his lone remaining stick while the other weaves its haphazard path back to him.

Kate takes her eyes off Linc for a moment. She smiles. "It's all perfect."

We walk home under the cloud-scudding sky. Johnny's hand is warm in mine, his eyes teasing as he kisses me under a streetlight. We pass a particular picket fence and I pick a flower from the garden for my hair.

"You know Mel and Dave are the only people in Mayton who grow hellebores that colour."

"No, really?" My hand goes instinctively to remove the bud.

His smile quirks. "No."

"Don't scare me like that!"

"You could stop taking flowers from people's gardens." At the suggestion, I give him a Look and he grins. "I know, what was I thinking?"

I twist in his arms and kiss him. "Johnny, I want to ask you something."

"Go ahead."

"Will you stay with me?"

"Whenever you like."

"I mean forever. Will you move in with Doris and I?"

"I don't know. I was thinking of moving back into the Station."

I think he is joking, but... "Consider it? I want see you every day. I want to have breakfast with you, and dinner, and... other things." Mm. Other things. "Of course, I know it's a bit sudden. And it means you'll also have to live with Clyde and my nonagenarian step-grandmother, which I realise might be..."

He laughs, deep and warm. "Relax, sunshine, of course I want to be with you."

I toss my flower at him. "I can't promise we'll be here forever. Shirley is great friends with Doris and a big support so I might decide to travel again for a bit, or go live in a tree, you know?"

"I know." Johnny's handsome face is glowing.

"But you can come too."

"That sounds good." He wraps his arms around me.

"By the way, I'm going to open a record store."

"In Mayton?"

"Yes, right next to Billie's shop."

"You'll be good at that, Quinn. You could sell pasta to Italians."

I snuggle close. I promise myself that tomorrow, I will reach out to Az. I am feeling charitable, she has been my friend since forever and it was perhaps precipitous of me to block her without discussion. And I will hang up the ink drawings of young Alfred and his dog, and the Fire Station horses. I will find somewhere pride of place in the cottage, so they can be seen by everyone who visits and we can enjoy them every day.

Idly, I follow another thought. "And soon you'll meet my mother and I'll meet your mamma and we'll get married. What do you think?"

"I think, Quinn, that when you get ideas I just do as I'm told." Johnny's voice is a caress. "I love you."

"I love you, too."

"Kiss me, bella." *In Fire Station Lane.*

I lift my face for Johnny's kiss.

There comes a wild tooting behind me. Billie is hanging out the window of Lollie's car, Brad's hand at her waist to stop her falling out. "Woo hoo, loversh in the lane (hic), hey Quinn, let's climb that oak tree at your place. I wanna see if I can do it. Come on Lollie, drive me round there."

"No way," Lollie objects, "Milly's paint will get scratched. I saw that dent in the back of Johnny's fire truck after he..."

"But he hit the fence (hec) I'm just arsh- asking you to take me to the end of the lane."

Brad intercedes. "Billie, darling, you've been drinking, let's go home and..."

"Bradley Evans just (hic) one liddle climb. What dish-, desh-, destructible thing could happen?"

"Lots," I say.

"Paperwork," says Johnny.

Billie pouts. "But Quinn climbs that tree all the time. I reckon from up there (hic) we'll see Wellington."

"You can't see Wellington." Johnny is adamant.

"Well, I'm good at climbing now (hic) so Quinn, don't shtand there being boring and sensible, kissing Johnny." A pause. "Acshually though, I can understand you wanting to shtand there and..."

"Billie!"

"But Bradley Evans, you gotta admit he's sizzling hot."

While they squabble in the back of the Mini Countryman, I look at Johnny. "I hate being called boring and sensible."

A wing lifts. "I doubt it happens often."

"My oak tree is very good for climbing."

His gaze holds mine. "I think Billie is a public menace. But I also know how much you love trees."

I feel sparkly all over. "I love you."

"Bella." Johnny kisses me, to more wolf whistles and applause from the car. He scoops me up and bundles me into the passenger seat next to Lollie. "Don't die. I want to marry you."

Lollie is tooting and cheering, and Billie joins in. "We're going climbing! Bradley darling, this time (hec) you better take my photo."

"Glory." I look back at Johnny as the Mini bumps up the kerb.

His smile quirks. "I'll bring the truck."

Acknowledgements

The *Mayton Hearts* series would not exist without the advice and camaraderie of my local romance writers group, the support of my husband (with that glint in his eye), and clever critique of my mum, extended family and friends. Thankyou, as always!

I owe my daughter and her wicked sense of humour for the delightful line, "I have a husband but it's not serious. There's room for one more."

I've had a lot of fun writing Quinn, with her forthright, hectic attitude to life. Johnny's firefighting adventures are purely fictional; Mayton is not a real town so I've taken a lot of creative licence, all errors in the way a fire station is usually run or an emergency response undertaken are mine alone.

Mayton's musos are channelled from my many years playing in bands – I find no matter where you are or what genre you play, there's always a diva, there's always expensive gear stuck together with tape, and there's always a Dave. He can play pretty much every instrument *and* do the lighting and sound. Thanks, Dave!

Lastly, a big thankyou to my readers. Look for more Abigail Bay books soon!

Did you love *Kiss Me in Fire Station Lane*? Then you should read *Come Back to Bed, Beautiful*[1] by Abigail Bay!

[2]

Kate Dale moved to the country for a fresh start, not to fall in love. But ever since tall, dark, handsome Linc Brady nearly ran her over with his truck she's been unable to think straight. His flashing smile and capable hands are a big distraction. It's a pity that Kate isn't looking for a man, and Linc is already taken. Or is he?

Linc Brady has no problem attracting women. His usual dilemma is how to avoid them. But this time he's fallen hard for the one woman in town who doesn't want him.

---

1. https://books2read.com/u/m0EJLJ

2. https://books2read.com/u/m0EJLJ

Meanwhile Kate is on a journey of healing, reconnecting with her sister Lori, and writing her bodice-ripping bestseller. She has no time for horses, a crumbling old farmhouse and small-town misunderstandings. Definitely no men! But could these be her secret to finding joy – and another chance at love?

A warm and addictive novel about sisters, friendship and slow burn romance, in a small town full of big characters.

Mayton Hearts, Book 1

Read more at https://www.abigailbay.com.

Also by Abigail Bay

Mayton Hearts
Come Back to Bed, Beautiful
Kiss Me in Fire Station Lane

Watch for more at https://www.abigailbay.com.

About the Author

Abigail Bay writes about people, animals, and the gorgeous, messy mayhem of life and love. She has also written scientific papers, short stories and songs. Abbie lives with her family in a bushclad valley in Aotearoa New Zealand.

Read more at https://www.abigailbay.com.